AF413168

MY BROTHER'S KEEPER

My Brother's Keeper

VICTOR M. SANDOVAL

Pasadena, California

Dedication

To my wife, LuAnn, who read every draft

and

My sister, Maya, for her encouragement

"The King will reply, 'Truly I tell you, whatever you did for one of the least of these brothers and sisters of mine, you did for me.'

-Matthew 25:40

Chapter 1

I know some things about myself, but there's a lot I don't know about myself. I know I was named after my uncle, Edmundo Santos. My mother calls me Mundo. My mother says it means the world. She says I am the world, to her anyway. Everybody else calls me Ed or Eddie. I was born with a cord around my neck, so I couldn't breathe. I was choking to death. Dad says the doctors saved me. My Mother says God saved me. I don't know. When they tell the story about how I almost died at birth, they tell everyone I was a "CP" baby, that I have Cerebral Palsy. I don't know what that means. All I know is that all my life I've noticed that people, people I know, people I don't know, seem to always have some secret among themselves that they don't share with me. It's the way they smile when they're around me, like I got the mumps or something and I don't know it. Like they feel sorry for me. But I don't feel sorry for myself. I do the best with what I got like my father taught me. But with grown-ups, it's always the same.

"And this is my oldest son, Edmundo," Dad says to my counselor at Arroyo High School. It's my first day after the last bell. Around a small table with us sit the school psychologist, the nurse, the principal, a reading specialist, my home room teacher, and some other school people, too. Our knees hit together under the table when our chairs are pulled up close. "I want him in all the same classes that my other sons have. No different. I don't want him in special classes."

"But Mr. Santos, you don't understand, we've tested Ed . . . ," the school psychologist starts to speak. "Using the latest 1980 programs . . . ."

"I don't understand? You don't understand." Dad gets red in the face. "This is my eldest son, the head of the house after me. He does everything with his brothers. Wherever they go they take care of him, he takes care of them. Mundo studies all the time. Give him the grade he earns. Good or bad. That's okay, but he's not going into any special program where nobody cares about him."

"We all, all of us here, know it's hard bringing up a handicapped child, but Mr. Santos, please," the school nurse says.

"You do?" Dad cuts her off. "Then you know he needs to be with all sorts of kids, not just the ones you call 'special.' When he was little, we kept him home. We didn't want him to go to school. We didn't want him to be made fun of. When he did go to school, they held him back a few grades, but now he's going to high school with his brothers. He won't miss a day. He'll behave. He's a nice boy."

"Mr. Santos, may I ask Eddie something?" says Miss Glass, my home room teacher, already my favorite teacher.

"Yes, okay." My father looks surprised by her soft, kind voice.

"Hi, Eddie." She smiles at me like in class. "Eddie what do you want to do? Stay here at Arroyo or attend Marshall High for special education students?"

"Me? What do I want?" I say, hearing my voice like it belongs to someone else. "I want to be here with my brothers. I want to be on the school cross-country team with them. At home we practice all the time. I run with them in the hills around our house. We have fun together. They run ahead of me and sometimes I'm left behind, especially running up the steep hills, but it's okay. They wait at the top for me. Yeah, I like that. They're my brothers and they want me to be there with them. No matter what, just laughing, joking around, running, or just sitting quiet, doing nothing. They accept who I am. How I am. That's what I want."

"Thank you, Eddie," says Miss Glass.

Finally, the Principal, Mr. Gonzales, says that I can remain at Arroyo under certain conditions. First, I must maintain a "C" average. Second, no discipline problems. Third, because I've been held back from entering school for two years, I will be a sophomore at eighteen years old and will be transferred next year to adult education classes to complete high school diploma requirements.

****

My father didn't listen to anyone. He told the doctors his first-born son was not going to be a cripple. From the very beginning, he protected me and wanted to reshape me. Every day after working in the trucking yards, he would lay me down on the living room floor and start exercising my left leg and arm, pulling them straight and forcing them to move like pistons or springs. I would try not to cry, but the pain made me scream out, "No more, Daddy. No more, please." He just kept on. Sweat (or was it tears?) streamed from his face, soaking my t-shirt. I could see my mother in the kitchen holding her hands over her ears and crying.

You'd think he'd let up after he had Jesse, a strong healthy boy, but it didn't work that way. I was the oldest, and he expected a lot from me because of it. As though by sheer will, he fathered two more boys in quick succession, Jaime, Jorge. All healthy and strong. But it wasn't enough, he wanted me to lead the way.

When I turned fourteen, he took me to Ray's gym on First Street where amateur boxers trained. He told Ray, a tattooed, muscular boxer with a melted wax nose, to get me in the ring, to let me know what it was like. At first Ray refused, "He's got only one good arm and one good leg. What's the point?"

But father insisted, "He's got to learn to take care of himself. Put him in with one of the eighteen-year-olds. Tell them not to hold back."

"Okay, he's your kid."

They put the gloves on me, no protection, and pushed me into the ring. My opponent was tall and had muscles well shaped from daily weightlifting. At first, I could see he didn't really want to fight me. He saw my left arm limp at my side and my slow steps forward, dragging a twisted foot.

"Go on, hit him!" Father said. "It's okay. He's my son. Do it. Hit him."

And the guy did. Punch after punch, to my head, eye, cheek, and nose. Then came a blow to my jaw that knocked me down. I ran my glove across my mouth and a red streak appeared. My mouth was bleeding.

"Get up!" Father was shouting. "Get up, Mundo. Get up!"

I didn't want to, but I did. I turned to my right side and got to my feet. Then, before I could take another blow, my father was in the ring, positioned himself between us and grabbed my shoulders.

"Good. You did good," he said.

Thinking about it at home later, I knew my father wasn't trying to hurt me on purpose. It did hurt. But I knew he loved me and wanted me to be able to walk and run and play like all the other kids. So, I tried my best. That's all I know; my father wanted me to try my best.

****

I remember my mother letting me stay home from school on my birthday when I was younger.

My father called her Prieta. She was a dark brown, Aztec-looking woman, with black hair that had white streaks on the sides, pulled back in a bun that was loose about the back of her neck.

"Sit at the table with me," she said. "I boiled the cauliflower and here is some butter to go with it."

We sat at the small dining room table across from one another and pulled sprigs or what my mother called "ramitas" from the head of the cauliflower and dipped them in the liquid butter.

"Es bueno." She looked at me with her green eyes set in a heart shaped face with high cheek bones. Her teeth were brown with decay on the edges, so she was embarrassed to smile and show them.

We sat for a while without talking, enjoying the cauliflower.

"Oh, we need more butter," she said. She moved quietly on small, tender feet, but seemed to hover above the ground, floating instead of walking, shuffling, instead of taking steps one at a time. She always wore an apron and was always in the kitchen cooking.

I knew, we all knew, that she expected the best from us, and if we screwed up, she would be disappointed, which would hurt us a lot. But we never gave her a reason to be ashamed of us because we knew how much she endured. When things seemed toughest, she stood strong and bent with the wind, but never broke.

****

Spic, beaner, cholo, Mexican, wet-back, in high school they call you all kinds of names, but I don't care. You get used to it, just don't call me Special Ed. I don't like it because if my brothers found out, well, that person would wish he never said it.

In homeroom, you know, the teacher will treat you best. Ms. Glass gives me extra time to finish tests and answer questions in class. She has a smile like a flashlight aimed at a dark corner.

She says, "Eddie, don't worry. Take your time." And smiles. Imagine? Sometimes she whispers in my ear, "I know your talk is slow, but your mind isn't. Don't give up."

In class, she knows that most of the time I know the answers to her questions, but the words don't come out just right. When some of the students laugh, it doesn't bother me. I know I'll keep trying to do my best no matter what.

I know how I look. I've seen myself in meet films. You know I run cross-country for the school team with my brothers, Jesse, and Jaime. I look like a desert tree on one side with my bony right shoulder, withered arm, and short leg all twisted like dry sticks, broken and stiff. But the other side is purrfect, a strong arm and a leg with muscles. But in every race, I always, always come in last.

I remember the first day going to the team tryouts for cross-country. My brothers, Jesse and Jaime, were already on the team, but they told the head coach, Mr. Ledesma, about me and how much I wanted to be on the team, too.

"Have him show up," Mr. Ledesma said. "He can try out just like anybody else."

The following Monday I was there at the school field for tryouts.

"I'm Mr. Ledesma. But you can call me coach Led," he said, smiling as we, twenty or so freshman and sophomores, huddled around him. "Okay, this is the deal. If you want to make the team you've got to run the two-mile course. Period. If you can do that, you've made the team."

"How fast?" Someone called out. "Is there a time limit? Do we have to run it in a certain time?"

"No time limit. If you can run the two miles, you're on the team," said coach Led.

After twenty minutes of warm up time, coach Led called out, "Everybody, toes on the line. Start at my whistle. Okay, ready." Then a blast from his whistle started us running to the dirt path that began the course surrounded by tall bushes and trees, the start of the two-mile run.

At first, I was running along behind with a few other freshmen stragglers. But after a while I found myself running alone, last, and coughing up a lot of dust. It didn't bother me. I knew all I had to do was finish the course. And I knew I could do that even with my twisted foot. I knew it would take me some time, longer than everybody else. And I did wonder if the coach would keep his word, "there's no time limit."

When I came out at the end of the course, the other runners were there holding their sides and catching their breath. Some were fully rested and sitting on a bench drinking Gatorade. I hobbled toward them in silence. Then I felt a pat on my back. I looked around and saw coach Led.

"Congratulations! Welcome to the team," said coach Led, loud enough for everyone to hear.

****

I get lonely sometimes. There's no music in my life, not like in the movies. You know what I mean, when the movie star hero kisses the beautiful girl, the violins and other stringed instruments begin to play. When the bad guys are near and ready to pounce, the hero is surrounded by deep bass sounds of drums or piano keys. I like that. But there's no music like that in my life. I live each moment without the help of a song. Well, maybe sometimes I do make my own music. Sometimes I whistle to help me pass the time or to not feel alone. I whistle a lot, otherwise there's no music in my life.

Oh, I have friends. Jimmy's my best friend. He runs cross-country, too. And I remember the other day he saved me, big time. It was between classes when I went to the restroom.

"What you doing here sophomore?" Three football players in letterman's jackets stared at me. "Don't you know this is a senior restroom, just for seniors?" They pinned me against the wall. I knew what they said was a lie just to make trouble.

I made a fist with my good hand and flexed my muscles on my good arm. I was ready for them.

Then Jimmy walked into the restroom, seeing the footballers grabbing my shirt and pushing me hard against the tile.

"Hey, what you guys doing?"

"What's it to you? You gonna do something about it?"

"No, not me." Jimmy walked up to the mirror and casually combed his hair. "But his brothers will."

"Oh, yeah, I'd like to see that."

"No, you wouldn't. One is a junior, the other a senior. And they'll kick your ass so far down the street, you won't find your way home."

The three crew cuts exchanged looks of pure concentration, like solving a math problem.

"Just saying . . . ," Jimmy turned from the mirror and put his comb in his pocket.

"He's not worth it. Let's get out of here." They brushed by Jimmy, giving him an elbow in his ribs.

After they left, Jimmy straightened up my shirt.

"Are you Okay?"

"Sure, I was ready for them."

"I know. I know. One punch from that fist of yours, he would've been down. But you know your brothers don't want you to fight and get into trouble. It'll get you kicked out of the school. You'll have to go to Marshall High where they send . . . you know. Your dad wouldn't like that."

"Yeah, you're right." I put my arm around his narrow shoulders and squeezed him.

"Hey, not too tight." Jimmy looked up at me. His deep brown hair was curly in places. He was the smallest guy on the team, but he could run. "Have you been working out with weights?"

"No, Jimmy, sorry, my dad says I don't know my own strength."

****

I don't hate school. But I don't like school.

I remember in the first grade, my teacher, a brand new teacher, announced that today we were going to start preparing for "Open House." She explained this is when all the parents come to see the work their children have been doing in school. So I was very excited because I knew that my abuelita would come to see my school work. Now, my abuelita was a stout woman with long, braided black hair who dressed in bright colors and wore red lipstick. She worked every day at the central market downtown selling vegetables. But I knew she would take time off for me.

Sometimes on Saturdays she would let me help her at the market. I would stand on a wooden box next to her as people picked out fruit and vegetables from the baskets arranged in front of her covered stall. I would get the folded brown paper bags, snap them open in the air, and people would fill them with their choices. All the while abuelita would be talking to them in Spanish and some broken English too, and, at the same time, in her mind counting out the cost.

Our assignment for today, the teacher said, was to draw an apple, the prettiest apple we've ever seen. She put color pencils and crayons and small dishes of tempura paint on our desks. We all had these plastic aprons we wore to protect our clothes.

I liked to draw. I took my time and closed my eyes so I could picture just the right apple to draw for my abuelita. Then I began to draw with pencils and a touch of paint. When I was finished, I was very happy with my apple. I knew my abuelita would like it, too. Then the teacher came around to everyone's desk, praising them about this or that in their apple drawings. But when she came to my desk, she looked at my drawing, then looked at me in the face with a horrible look. Like, I did something wrong.

"Eddie look around the room at what all the other students have drawn. They drew apples, red apples," she said.

I looked around the room at all the red apples spread out on the desks around me.

"Your apple is yellow. Eddie, apples are red," she said. "Here take the red tempera paint and color out all the yellow and you'll be fine. It will be just like everyone else's." And she put the brush with red paint in my hand and guided it over my drawing of my apple, making it red.

I pulled my hand out of hers and ran out of the room crying and heard her calling, " Eddie, Eddie come back. It's all right." It wasn't all right. She ruined my abuelita's golden apple.

On "Open House" day, my abuelita made me go with her even though when I came home crying, I told her about my yellow apple. She said we had to go.

"I don't have anything to show." I tried to explain to her that the apple, the red apple with my name on it wasn't my apple. I drew a yellow apple.

When we arrived at the school the principal gave a short speech in the auditorium, then sent us all to each of our teachers' classrooms. I showed her to my classroom. When we went in, my teacher stood there, greeting everyone. She smiled at us. My abuelita shook her hand and smiled back. We walked around the room and looked at all the student displays, then looked at all the pictures the students had drawn of apples that were pinned on the bulletin boards along the walls. Finally, when my abuelita came to the picture with my name on it, she stood silently there for a while. Then she said in a soft voice, " Es un Durada Deliciosa, magnifico, Eddie."

When we were about to leave my abuelita took me by the hand. We went up to the teacher who was standing next to her desk. As we came near, my abuelita reached into her woven hemp bag and pulled out a yellow apple that she gave to me and said, "Deces tu maestra gracias y dar esta manzana. Y dil a ella es un Dorada Deliciosa."

I did as I was told. I said to the teacher, "Thank you. Here is an apple for you. It is called a Golden Delicious."

The teacher took the apple from my hand and stared at it, lost, puzzled. We turned and walked slowly out the door, smiling at each other, my abuelita and me.

Chapter 2

I sit quietly in my second period Spanish class. It's my favorite because Mr. Ledesma is my Spanish teacher. Mr. Ledesma is my cross-country coach, too. Everyone calls him coach Led. He is a tall, lanky, six-footer who ran track for USC where he graduated and was a star runner. He has close-cropped black hair and large ears. He said that his ears were like large sails that helped him run faster. Almost everything is comical to him. He likes to joke a lot. Not the kind of joke that hurts or targets someone, but he can tell very funny stories.

We all learn a lot of Spanish, but we also learn a lot about life from the stories coach Led likes to tell. He likes the focused attention of all of us as he tells tales about growing up poor, about working hard, and finding that the loneliness of the long-distance runner is true. He laughs. Running, he says, is his therapy. He loves being out in the open, looking at the blue sky, and feeling a cool wind rush across his dark skin. I know he is somebody that I could go to if I ever had a problem.

The only student in the class that notices me is Sandra. She's a tall, gawky, dark-haired Junior who is part of the cheerleading team.

She knows I speak Spanish, so she often asks me about certain words and sentences. I don't mind. She is nice. Whenever she sees me on campus, no matter how far away, she waves at me and yells, "Hi, Eddie!"

Once I asked her why she was so nice to me. She said, "Because you remind me of somebody I know."

"Who?" I asked.

"Me," she said.

"What?"

"When I first started high school, I was like you, shy and didn't have any friends. So, I decided I'd be your friend."

We've been friends ever since.

"Do you know," I say to her as we sit with our desks next to each other. "No one comes out for the cross-country meets. I mean, there's no cheerleaders. There's a drill team, cheerleaders, and a band for football and basketball games. Cross-country has nothing. Why?"

Sandra scrunches her face, arches her eyebrows, and says, "I don't know, but you're right. There should be someone there cheering you on just like the other sports."

"Do you think so?" We look at each other for a while in silence.

"I'm gonna ask about it. I'm going to do something about it," Sandra says. " I don't know about the others, but I'll get some of my friends on the cheerleading team to be at one of your meets. I promise."

****

"Okay, guys listen up," coach Led hollers. His voice echoes through the locker room where all of us sit, putting on our running shoes. "You know we've got a big meet on Saturday. Now, you know me, I'm not going to yell at you or pound the lockers to make a point."

We all stop what we were doing and give him all our attention. All the team members are eager to practice at the end of the school day.

"You are a team," coach Led says. "There's no prima-donnas here. We work together. That's why we win. And think about this, we have the home course advantage. You guys know where the steep hills are and where the down slopes begin. You let the down slope speed you up and around the corner you expect the climb. You know the course better than anyone. But to win, we must work to-gether as a team."

Looking around the room, I can see everyone is serious and quiet.

"So, this is what we're going to do for practice today. I want each of you to be a pace-setter. You know what I mean. Every five hundred yards the lead runner drops back, the next one up takes the lead, and sets the pace. Ques-tions? Then let's do it." Coach Led stretches out his arm with an open hand.

We all stand up, circle him, put our hands on top of his and yell, "Go, Eagles!"

Our two-mile and three-mile courses are a lot different than most schools. We have this huge cement flood channel running along the edge of our school. We call it the arroyo. It has steep dirt embankments on either side covered with all sorts of bushes, plants, weeds, and small trees. This is our running course for practice and for meets. The narrow path is well marked and well traveled, but of course you must watch out for roots sticking out of the ground, strewn rocks the size of cantaloupes, and sometimes snakes. So, we look out for each other because all the arroyo growth hides us from view. No one can see the runners on the course. The coach and officials see us go into the brambles at the start, then see us come out of the brambles on the other end.

We have about twenty-five runners total. That's three teams—Varsity, Junior Varsity, Frosh/Soph. Each school's team needs at least five runners to compete, but most have seven or more.

My brothers, Jesse, and Jaime are on the Varsity and Junior Varsity teams. I'm on the Frosh/Soph team with Jimmy. When it's our turn to go , we put our toes on the line and wait for coach Led to blow the whistle. When he does, we start as a clump of runners, shoulder to shoulder, heading toward the bramble path, but soon after, we pace ourselves one after the other in a single line. Of course, I'm the last runner by a long shot. It doesn't bother me. Coach Led says that I'm an inspiration and motivation for the whole team. I know by running last I'm not hurting the team because only the first five finishers count to score. Each finisher earns a number, first place equals one, second place equals two. You know what I mean. So, the team with the lowest combined score wins the meet. But each team must have five team members cross the finish line, if not, the team forfeits the race.

Today, as I run and try to move forward, I feel like I have lots of gum stuck to my shoes, both of them. But that doesn't stop me. I'll never quit trying. I love to run. It's great to be part of a team. I try hard to run faster, but I can hardly move, as if strings of pink chewing gum cling to my leather shoes, making it hard to move without wishing that I could climb out of my shoes and fly like there's no tomorrow.

The tall patch of milkweed marks the end of the half mile stretch. I keep running. When I see the small palo verde tree that blooms yellow flowers in the spring, I know I'm at end of the of the first mile. I keep running. When I see the stand of castor bean canes with many-fingered leaves, I know I hit the one-and-three-quarter mile mark.

That's when I see one of the first-year kids on the ground in front of me. He is lying on the ground, on his side, reaching for his ankle.

"What happened? Are you Okay?" I say as I kneel down beside him.

"I tripped on something," he says. "I can't get up. I can't walk."

"It's okay. I can help you." I put my arm around his shoulder. "Do you want to try and stand up with my help? We're not too far from the finish."

"Okay, I'll try."

"Easy does it. Your name is Glenn, right?" I remember this skinny freshman right away as I hold on to him while he manages to get upright. "Do you think you can make it with my help?"

"Yeah, I think so." Glenn put his weight on his right leg and lifted his left ankle above the ground.

I brace him on my strong right side and together we slowly hobble to the finish line. My team is there sitting on the benches, drinking Gatorade, and, like always, waiting for me to finish. They didn't realize Glenn was missing until they see both of us struggle out of the bramble.

"Louie, go get the nurse." Coach Led is the first one to rush toward us. He sits Glenn on the ground. "Somebody get me some ice from the cooler and a towel."

Coach Led knows exactly what to do. He puts the ice on Glenn's ankle, then looks up at me and says, "Good job, Eddie. You did a good job."

My brothers and other team members come up to me and pat me on the back and even offer me some cold Gatorade.

When the nurse comes with a stretcher crew, she looks at Glenn's ankle. "He'll be all right. It's only a sprained ankle, but it will take a few days."

Glenn smiles up at me. Then the nurse comes toward me.

"Eddie, I heard you were the one who carried him home," she says. "Well done."

The nurse knows my name.

****

In my room in bed, I stare up at the ceiling. I remember dreams. Sometimes I wake up at night between the fog of sleep and the darkness of closing dreams. I remember in my dream, seeing a glint of light bouncing from a shell button on my mother's sweater when I was three. I remember the tobacco smell of my father's breast pocket where he kept his Camels.

I remember little things, instant, first things, which are as real and bold as an exploding star a million miles away, that only I can see in my dreams.

"Ring, ring, ring." It's the alarm. I jump out of bed and put on my clothes and boots. I'm ready to go to work. My brothers not so much. We all sleep in the same room. I see them roll to one side and hear them moan.

"Come on guys," I say. "We don't wanna be late. We gotta get out of here by six o'clock."

It's Saturday morning and our work at Sunny View car wash will start soon. My brothers slowly get out of bed, go to the closet, and put on their gray uniforms. Finally, they pull on their black boots and tuck their shirts into their pants.

Like always, we smell the bacon frying in the kitchen as our mother makes our breakfast. When she calls us, we sit around our large kitchen table as she brings plates of bacon, scrambled eggs, and beans that she puts in front of us. I sit at the head of the table. That is my place. My brothers are a loud bunch. They eat large mouthfuls, and, at the same time, crack jokes, punch each other's shoulders, and laugh.

When we finish eating, we pile into Jesse's old jalopy. He drives us to Sunny View's front gate which is still closed because we are early. He parks and we all slump over in our seats, close our eyes, and wait for the gates to open.

After the gates open, we drive in, park, and get out of the car. We go straight to our stations. Each of us has a different responsibility when it comes to washing and putting the cars through the tunnel that shoots water, soap, and air, leaving a clean, dry car at the end of the track, finished.

I go straight to the dryer and pull out all the towels and rags that we use to clean, wash, and dust. The rags are color-coded. I sort them into large canvas bags stretched on a wheeled metal frame. We use white towels to clean the inside and outside of the car, including the windows. The red rags are for road tar on the wheel wells and the tire rims. When I'm finished sorting, I roll the canvas bags to the three places at the beginning, middle, and end of the car tunnel. While I'm working, the other guys are laughing, joking, punching each other, bobbing and weaving.

I hear Jesse and Jaime place bets on who will get the most tips that day. Each one of them has his little secret way of pleasing a customer. Jesse likes to tell jokes and make people laugh. Jaime knows that customers like to have their rearview mirror cleaned and put back in the exact same place they left it.

My youngest brother, Jorge, is in middle school, but he passes for a high schooler. His job is to get into the car just before the huge blow dryer sweeps over with high velocity air. He then sprays window cleaner and wipes the windows clean from the inside. Before the car is free of the conveyor track, he finishes all the windows and then jumps out of the car. The rest of us dry off any remaining water droplets and our supervisor drives the car off.

We put in about ten hours a day, but don't complain because the money is good. Of course, we give some to our mom, but the rest we get to spend on whatever we like.

****

On Sundays we go to church, my mom, me, and my brothers. Dad doesn't go because mom says he's mad at God for what he did to me and what he did to his older brother, Edmundo, who has polio.

After church, me and my brothers drive up to the nearby hills, Las Lomas, to run on the ridge to keep in shape. But before we run, we park on gravity hill. Jesse turns off the engine and points us downhill without the brake, so we thought. But in a minute or two the car starts rolling backwards uphill. It's like a huge horseshoe magnet is pulling us from behind. When I ask my brothers about it. They all say, "Gravity, I guess. Anyway, things aren't always what they seem."

After running the trails for an hour, we sit on the road guard rail to rest and to spy on him. El Indio lives about a hundred feet below us in an open flat area where he guards a big warehouse surrounded by a chain-link fence. Me and my brothers heard about El Indio long before we ever saw him. The guy who owns the warehouse pays El Indio to watch over the place, like a security guard or something, but he doesn't pay El Indio with money. He pays him with vegetables, you know, heads of lettuce, celery, watermelons, cantaloupes, tomatoes, beans, and rice. That kind of stuff. El Indio is vegetarian, I guess. Everyone in the barrio could tell you a story about El Indio chasing kids away with his blood-dripping machete that would have you running home to your mama real fast.

The very first time we saw El Indio, we were resting at the top of the ridge looking down. Below us, where the warehouse stood, we saw El Indio, short and muscular, let a car drive in through the fence gate. A man in a gray suit got out of the car, shook El Indio's hand, and pointed to the trunk.

They went to the back of the car, opened the trunk, and El Indio got these one-gallon paint cans out. He carried them over to the warehouse. After a while, the man drove away. El Indio locked the gate and began painting, "No Trespassing," in big letters on a piece of wood. When he finished, he pounded a stake into the ground and nailed the sign to it. Then he began to paint all the outside concrete walls of the warehouse white.

We sat there and laughed. We were all thinking the same thing. Those white walls will be covered with graffiti in no time. But after we thought about it, we realized no one would dare with El Indio on guard with his machete. After weeks of work, El Indio left the empty paint cans stacked in the open inside the gate. In time, somehow, the whole neighborhood thought this was a clever way to get rid of their used cans of paint, so they left them near the gate so El Indio could find them. They thought they were getting the better part of the deal, more room in the garage and an offering to soothe the crazy man with a machete. What a deal. After all, half empty cans of paint are like crusty scabs on cuts that once served a purpose, but now, after you peel them off you don't know how to get rid of them. Sure enough, El Indio eventually stacked the abandoned paint cans inside the fence near the warehouse.

****

Believe me, the first time I met El Indio face to face was very scary. One morning I got up early before daylight, before my brothers were awake. I wanted to see for myself if El Indio did have a machete "as long as your arm and as sharp as your mother-in-law's tongue." That was what everyone said anyway. So, I jumped out of the bedroom window and headed to Las Lomas, just above the lot where El Indio lived and worked. I sat in the tall, damp grass surrounded by mustard weeds. I focused my eyes on his trailer, just below. It really wasn't a trailer, but instead a camper shell. The kind that was made to fit into the back of a pickup truck. But El Indio didn't have a truck, so the camper shell stood on metal legs about two feet off the ground, looking like a crab. Neat.

As daylight drifted in from behind my shoulder, I waited and waited for movement, for El Indio to come out. I must have fallen asleep for awhile because a loud sound woke me up, "thwap," metal against wood. I looked down the hill and saw El Indio standing in front of his camper next to a table made of a sheet of plywood with sawhorses for legs. His white teeth flashed beneath his thin mustache as he swung a huge silver blade from above his head, down across a head of cabbage, slicing it in two equal parts, "thwap." Dios mío!

El Indio was thin and ageless. I mean I couldn't tell if he was my age or sixty. He moved like a young person, but his face was old. His eyes were deep in his head and sad. His head of long black hair was tangled and knotted, the least of his worries. But this I can tell you: he knew how to cut up vegetables with a machete like I've never seen.

Anyway he started to sing as he chopped, in Spanish, I think, or maybe it was some other language. It was hard to tell from a distance. After awhile he sat down on an old wooden crate and lifted a jug of water to his lips, then poured some over his head to cool off.

Then it happened. As I moved my foot for balance, a rock broke loose and started tumbling down the hill. El Indio looked up and saw me. His eyes met mine and I was scared. I stood up to run, but my feet slipped under me and I fell down the hill. I was sliding down head first on my stomach across the dewy grass really fast. When I finally stopped, El Indio had a clump of my hair in one hand and his machete in the other. All I could do was to close my eyes and hold my hands up to guard my face.

"Quieres agua?" he asked.

"What?"

"Do you want some water to drink?"

"What? Yeah. Sí, sí."

He let go of my hair and helped me to my feet as he led me to his camper and the jug of water.

"What's your name?" El Indio passed me the jug to drink.

"Eddie, Edmundo. Everyone calls me Eddie," I said. "What's your name?" I looked at him and could see he was a young man, not much older than me.

"The name everyone calls me, you know it."

"What? Oh, El Indio?"

"Sí, El Indio. Why not. That's what I am."

That's how we met each other. From then on, as long as I come by myself, I'm welcome to visit El Indio.

Chapter 3

I visit El Indio a lot, sometimes after school even, but mostly on weekends after church. Like today, I run up the paved road that snakes through Las Lomas to the lot surrounded by a chain-link fence. When he sees me there, El Indio unlocks the gate and lets me in. We just sit, talk, and eat some raw vegetables that he puts together.

"Do you guard this lot and warehouse?"

"Yeah, that's what I do," El Indio says. "For over a half a year now since I left my home."

"How did you end up here?"

"I was offered work here."

"Who hired you?"

"Mr. Peterson. Oh, it's a long story. He needed me here to make sure that his warehouse isn't . . . ? Comó dices? Vandalize? He wants to sell it."

"Is anything in it?"

"No, not a thing. Nada." El Indio stands up and motions for me to follow him as he walks toward the large cement-walled warehouse about the size of my high school gym. He unlocks the door. "Aquí, here, take a look inside."

As I step through, the sunlight floods in from the sky-lights. To the right, a door is open to a restroom with a shower, toilet, and sink. Then I see wooden shelves on my left stacked with one gallon paint cans, about forty of them.

"What do you do with all that paint?"

"Look around," he says. " Mirá, the wall at the back."

As my eyes get used to the light, I can see a huge colorful mural of mountains, trees, and trails. A cloudy light blue sky caps a forest in different shades of green, orange, and red that covers the entire twenty-foot-high wall of the warehouse.

"You did that?"

"Yeah, comó no. I needed something to do and I miss my home, the place where I was born."

"You lived in the mountains?"

"Sí, Copper Canyon, where I grew up and ran, and ran, and ran, up and down those canyon trails."

"Wow!"

"I use the paint left over in the old cans that people leave by the gate for me. Mostly I use the colors straight from the can. But sometimes I mix colors, yellow with blue or red with green, to get the trees and bushes exactly right."

"Beautiful. It's really beautiful."

"Sí, Como no. I lived in the village near Creel, high in the mountains. The Spaniards named them the Tarahumara Range. So, they called my people the Tarahumara because we lived there. But my ancestors, Raramuri, have lived there forever, long before the Spaniards came. I miss my family, my mother and my sisters."

****

About a week later, I visit El Indio again. I tell him about how I run on my high school cross-country team with my brothers. He lets me know that he is a runner too, a long-distance runner.

"Really, like on a team?"

"No, all my people where I lived run all the time. We're all long-distance runners from the day we're born."

"What do you mean?"

His dark hard eyes look at me and he begins to tell his story about his life in Chihuahua, Mexico, in the city of Creel, high in Copper Canyon.

"My home in the canyon was a forest of pine trees, oaks, and rocky trails. Looking down from the ridge, I saw patches of green and bursts of red and yellow in the autumn. In, spring, the fields below were covered with wildflowers."

"I can see it." I say.

"I lived in a small hut with my brother and sisters near a lumber yard that made railroad ties. La Dueña and her daughter, Licha, owned it and the village store. La Dueña, a large woman with man-sized hands, barked orders at the men, her workers. No one talked back or gave her the evil-eye because she would give it right back along with your last paycheck. I remembered being five years old and stealing candy from the glass display case with a sliding door. As I tried to sneak the wrapped sweets into my pocket, La Dueña grabbed me by the hair and shook me by the shoulders so hard all the candy fell out of my pockets.

'Traveso, indio malo!' La Dueña shoved me out the door.

"My father, short and strongly built, was born in the valley of his ancestors, the Raramuri Indians, just below the high canyon ridges. He worked for La Dueña, cutting down trees, milling logs into railroad ties, and loading them onto railcars. The same job waited for me and my brother when we grew to manhood, Papa promised.

"Like I told you, my people are Raramuri which means 'the people of the swiftly running feet.' That's what we do.

We run. To go from one place to another meant to run from one place to another. All the boys of my village kicked a hard round tree root, like a ball, high into the air; then ran to where it landed and kicked it again, and again, moving it in the direction they wanted to go. Sometimes it was just down the path to the village center fountain, or sometimes to the next village miles away. The girls ran, too. They had sticks that they used to toss large wooden rings in the air as they ran along a path, headed to who knows where.

"When we were eight or nine, me and Chaparro ran for hours without stopping as we kicked the wooden ball up and down the canyon trails, running errands for our parents or La Dueña.

"Life went on like this until Papa's accident. On that day, several men and my father, the lead man, were working the railcar, loading the finished ties into straight rows with the help of a crane, evenly placing the weight across the bed of the railcar. Then, for some damn reason, one of the ties just did not fall into place and stuck out at one end. This would not do. Papa climbed onto the railway ties and tried to push it into place by jumping on it with the full weight of his body. But as the tie moved into place, his sandaled foot slipped along the fresh tar and became wedged between two ties. He hollered in great pain until the others could free him. But the damage was done, his ankle was broken in two places. He could not walk. This I swear."

"I believe you," I say as El Indio continues.

"La Dueña made sure he had the best doctor's care. But after spending much time changing plaster casts and hobbling on a makeshift crutch, my father never fully got the use of his leg back and could not do the job he had once done. Our family was left without a way to buy food or clothes, but we were grateful for our hut and being together.

"Then me and Chaparro tried to offer ourselves as helpers at any price to La Dueña, but she was worried, believing that another accident might happen.

'Your family would be better off planting corn in the fields to survive, rather than working for me,' she said as she cupped our chins in her large hands. 'Pobres.'

"So, we worked in the fields long hours, just barely earning enough to feed our family. Then the drought came. Everyone became desperate. There was no water for planting corn or anything else. I remember my father hobbled around in circles in the dirt as if he wished to disappear in a swirl of dust.

"It was August when the word went out that an American, Ralph Peterson, was offering money to anyone who would return with him to the U.S., to a place called Colorado, and run a race, a foot race of a hundred miles. The American was a sun-burnt, lean man. He said he was part of a charity in the U.S. that wanted to help us, the Raramuri. He knew about the drought and the many sick and starving people who needed help. He wanted to raise money to build a clinic for us.

So, he thought bringing in some of Raramuri runners who were known for their running endurance might help bring attention to our suffering and help with contributions. He would pay for all expenses, including the entry fees for the Colorado Leadville 100 mile-Marathon.

"I had prayed a lot for some help for my family. Strange as it was, this seemed to be God's answer. Me and Chaparro met with the tall man with a head of white-blonde hair and agreed to go with him to Colorado for the race. He paid my father some money, I don't remember how much, and promised him that he would take care of us and bring us back safely.

"Once there, in Colorado, everything seemed to go well. We were introduced from a high platform to a cheering crowd who looked at us with strange faces from underneath their hats. We bowed our heads and raised our hands, holding our home-made sandals high in the air. We would wear them to run the 100-mile race, a slab of old tire tread with leather lacing nailed to the edges that we tied around our feet and ankles. Ralph had given us new Nike running shoes, but we didn't want them. We wanted what we were used to.

"As we ran the race, many, many people lined the dusty road, shouting and yelling. Some handed out water in cups and oranges to suck on. The course took us through dusty trails, narrow rocky paths, and, sometimes, the hot, black pavement of the highway. After nearly twenty hours, just before noon on Sunday, me and Chaparro finished first and second across the finish line.

"For me and Chaparro, the Colorado run was a lot like running at home on the rugged trails of Copper Canyon where the air is clear and thin. We looked a lot alike. Not in the face, but in the way we ran. Mr. Peterson once said, 'We ran with the ease of deer and with gliding strides, like swans across the water.' We were about the same height, with rounded shoulders and muscular legs. From a distance, many friends and relatives mistook us one for the other."

"Where's your brother now?" I ask, but El Indio looks away and says no more.

****

At home alone in my room, I wonder what it would be like to live like El Indio in the mountains, to run in every direction, up and down steep cliff sides. I can tell that El Indio misses his family, friends, and running the mountain trails. The people of his village are all so far away. I wonder if he'll ever see them again. Will he ever return home? I am glad I have a home and a family, for sure.

I think about El Indio's brother, Chaparro. What happened to him? Where is he? I know brothers fight a lot. Did they have some kind of argument? Did Chaparro go home without his brother? I wonder.

Then, I begin to think about my father and Uncle Edmundo. When I was younger, about nine or ten, I went with my father to visit his older brother, Edmundo, every Saturday. Uncle Edmundo, broad chested, lived at the VA hospital on the west side. I remember the day we stopped going so often.

"You should be proud of your uncle," father said as he drove along the freeway. "Do you know he fought in WWII. He's a vet."

"What's a vet?" I asked.

"A veteran, mijo," father said. "He fought in Europe and survived. But when he got home, he got polio. Nobody could believe it."

"Polio?"

"That's why he has braces on his legs and is in a wheelchair."

When we arrived at the VA hospital, father parked in the lot. I followed him to the entrance where a man in a white shirt, led us to the large open area outside where lots of men were sitting on the benches, tables, and some in wheelchairs.

A bunch of guys surrounded my uncle, laughing and joking. When he spotted us across the lawn, he waved to us.

"How are you doing?" Father shook my uncle's hand.

"Great. I'm just doing great. It's good to see both of you." My uncle had a deep voice like a bass drum. He reached over, picked me up and sat me on his lap. "It's so good to see my little namesake, Edmundo. You're getting so big, tall like your dad."

Then, for the next couple of hours, I sat and listened to my father and uncle as they talked about old times when they were young.

"But you know, brother, that's the past," my uncle said. "This is today. I have a lot of friends here. We have good times. We look out for each other. You know you don't have to come every Saturday. I'm doing good here, enjoying myself, enjoying life. I have friends, books to read, and get plenty of good care."

"Yeah, I know, but . . . ."

"And you, Edmundo," my uncle said to me. "You must read, read every book you can get your hands on. Promise me you'll be a reader like me."

"I promise."

"Do you want me to tell you a war story?"

"Yes, yes!" I was excited. "About you in the war?"

"You want the long story or the short story?"

"The long one."

"Well, okay. When I was based in England as a bombardier, I went on a chow mission to Holland the day the war ended. My time spent there can be counted only in minutes, but the impression it made will last forever. About one o'clock that day, we flew across the English Channel. From the air, as on the ground, England is beautiful. The roads wind along through the unbelievably green fields.

"We hit the Channel at one thousand feet. The air was as smooth as silk. I rode all the way across the Channel in the tail turret. It hardly seemed possible the air would be so smooth. The day was warm, but the air was misty. The sea looked smooth, but one can't tell from above. At least there were no wind caps. We spent about forty minutes over the Channel.

"We could see the coast of Holland just a little while before we reached it. We immediately started descending. By the time we got to the coast we were quite low, and I had moved up to the pilot's compartment.

"At the coast it was easy to see the fortifications set up by the jerrys. There were huge anti-tank columns, pill boxes, gun mounts, with the ugly equipment sitting with their snoots in the air, useless. Believe me I was glad those guys had surrendered hours before.

"As we got farther inland there were fewer waterways, but still a lot. Along the highways were kids on bikes and others walking. They were only part of the picture. The older people were there, too. We could tell the difference. We must not have been more than one-hundred-fifty feet up from the ground. Everyone cheered and waved. A lot of them had flags. They were mostly Holland flags with the straight red, white, and blue stripes, but there were lots of American and English flags too. There were no cars on the roads. There were quite a few wagons all going in our direction. Later we found out why.

"The place we were going to drop our load, which I think was flour and beans, was about eight or ten miles south of Amsterdam. We could see that city to the left of us.

"The target was a huge field. From where I was, it looked like just a plain plowed field. I didn't look too closely though. I was watching the other planes dropping their food loads. We were about a hundred feet up.

"It was necessary to slow down as much as possible. So, as we approached, down went the wheels, flaps, and bomb bay doors. The pilot gunned the engines as much as possible. We were almost suspended in the air standing still. It was then I noticed thousands of people in carriages with horses, bicycles, or anything they had, lined up as far down the field as one could see.

"I looked into the bomb bays just as the load dropped. It went down and at least a few of the bags broke when they hit. Geez, it was a wonderful feeling to know that the food was going to people who really needed it. Eddie, never will I be able to describe the feeling that created. It almost justified my four years in the army to experience it. If what was in those sacks had been pure gold, no one in the airplane would have touched it. The people, on the ground along the way who were waving and jumping as we passed overhead, made us realize how much it meant to them, I felt.

"After the load dropped, the wheels went up, the flaps up, and bomb bay doors closed.

"We went so low that the altimeter read below zero, but we were about forty feet up. The Holstein cows ran in every direction. There were lots of them in the pastures. We came toward a church, directly ahead. I actually looked up at the steeple. We got around it all right sand headed back as low as was safe so we could see what there was to see.

"The whole time we were over Holland wasn't more than twenty-five minutes or a half hour. I was glad I was on board that day. The trip home was uneventful. I went back in the waist, the middle of the plane, and sat until we got back to the English coast. The sun was shining and made the trip from there inland very nice."

"I wish I could fly," I said, smiling at my uncle.

"Oh, you will one day, Eddie. Don't you worry."

"We'll see you next Saturday." Father shook my uncle's hand again as we began to leave.

"No, you won't, brother." My uncle would not let go of my father's hand. Then he lifted himself from the wheelchair and stood upright. "I don't want to see you spending time here when you could be with your wife and kids at home."

"Don't talk crazy," father said.

"I'm crazy? You only come to see me because you feel guilty for some reason. I don't know. But, brother, none of this, the way I am, is your fault."

"But you are my older brother," my father said. "I wanna be here for you."

"I know that, but you don't have to come every Saturday to prove it." My Uncle sat back down in his wheelchair, took a deep breath, and exhaled. "You know when I'm feeling down, I remember something I read a long time ago — "stuff that gets in the way is the way." It took me a long time to figure it out, but I got it. Every day I wake up happy because it is what it is, brother."

My father leaned over my uncle, and they hugged for a long time.

When father drove us home that day, I remember him whispering to himself, "stuff that gets in the way is the way."

I loved listening to my Uncle Edmundo's war stories. He told stories about people, strangers really, people he never met and how he helped them. He was glad that he was there to help them. When he was drafted, he was excited to think about flying in planes and shooting at the enemy. But, instead, he found the war a very sad thing. He said he came home a much humbler person than when he went into the service. I learned from him that helping other people makes you a better person.

****

In second period, after we settle down and open our books, coach Led calls my name and asks me to step outside with him.

I get up from my desk and follow him out the door to the hallway.

"How are you doing, Eddie?" coach Led says.

"Okay, I'm okay."

"Listen, the varsity football coach came to me yesterday." Coach Led leans in closer. "He said that some of his varsity players were complaining that you and your brothers were harassing them."

"What?"

"Yeah, something about threatening to beat them up. Did something happen between you guys?"

"No, nothing," I say. "The only thing that happened was that two varsity guys pushed me up against the wall in the bathroom the other day."

"And what happened?"

"Nothing, really, nothing."

"Come on, Eddie, something must have happened."

"Well, yeah, they were ready to beat me up when Jimmy came into the bathroom and told them to knock it off or my brothers would kick their asses."

"Oh."

"But coach, really nothing happened. They walked out the door. Jimmy can tell you that nothing happened. And I never told my brothers a thing. They don't know anything about it."

"Are you sure?"

"Yeah, I'm sure. I think those guys just want to make trouble. I don't want to get into trouble, and I don't want my brothers to get into trouble."

Coach Led looks me in the eyes and stays silent for a minute.

"If you don't believe me, ask Jimmy."

"No, no," coach Led says. "I believe you, Eddie. I believe you."

****

After class, Sandra walks with me down the hallway to our next class that we have together, Health and Safety.

"What was that all about?" Sandra asks. "What did coach Led say to you?"

"Oh, nothing, really," I say as I open the door to the classroom. Sandra sits in the front of the room and I sit at the back of the room. "I'll talk to you later."

Our Health and Safety teacher is also the drama teacher, Mr. Wilson. He is very showy in how he dresses and talks. He wears a purple beret to class. When he walks into the room, he whips it off his head and hangs it on the rack next to his desk.

"Okay, scholars," he says as he brushes the sides of his balding head to bring gray strands of hair over his small ears. "Today we have a special guest who will help us learn about CPR. Can anyone tell me what CPR means? What CPR stands for?"

Sandra raises her hand.

"Yes, Sandra, center stage. It's all yours."

"I think it means cardiopulmonary resuscitation."

"Ding, ding, ding, ding," Mr. Wilson yanks at an invisible rope tied to an invisible bell above his head. "The lucky lady is right again."

Everyone giggles a bit as Sandra stands up, curtsies and gives a bow.

"Okay, now let's get serious," Mr. Wilson says. "I want you to really pay attention to what you're learning today. And yes it will be on the final."

Everybody groans.

"Let's begin," he says as he stands in front of the class next to a six foot table with a blanket covering something underneath. "Let me introduce you to our special guest, Larry Lifesaver." Then he pulls the blanket off and we all see some sort of dummy, at least half of one. "Each of you is going to learn and practice the steps needed if someone you know or don't know suddenly has a heart attack."

The room grows silent.

"Larry, here, is going to be that person today. Get your books out, go to chapter twelve. Read and learn the steps of CPR. In about forty minutes after reviewing the text and memorizing the CPR instructions, each student will go to the front of the class and practice on Larry."

When it's my turn, I nervously stand beside Larry, the rubbery dummy. It has a man's head, face and chest, but no arms or legs.

"Okay what's the first thing you do?" Mr. Wilson says.

"Step one, you tap, and yell 'are you okay, can you hear me.' If there is no response, step two, you check to see if his chest is rising and falling. If he's not breathing, step three, you can try giving a thump to the middle of the sternum with your fist in a ball, tightened, using the heel of your palm where it meets your wrist. "

"Show me," he says.

I slam my fist hard on Larry's chest.

"Nice, not too hard now. You don't want to break a rib."

"Do this only once and then start the compressions," I say. "First, clasp your hands over the sternum and push down five times."

"Show me"

I position my hands, my strong hand on top of my other weak one, with fingers intertwined, and begin to push down.

"Then give Larry one breath," I say when I finished the compressions.

"For now, use your hand as a funnel." Mr. Wilson says. "Show me."

I watch for Larry's chest to rise after each breath.

"Good," Mr. Wilson says. "If Larry doesn't respond by movement or talking, you start with another five compressions and one breath. You should be able to finish ten cycles of compression and breaths in about two minutes."

I nod my head.

"Very good Eddie. That was a very good job. Okay, who's next? Remember we're practicing on Larry all week."

At the end of class Sandra and I walk out of the room, down the hall to her locker. I tell her about my talk with coach Led and what the varsity players said.

"I think they're trying to get me kicked out of school," I say. "Or maybe they think Jimmy is going to snitch on them. I don't know."

"Don't worry, Eddie," Sandra says. "Those guys can act like jerks sometimes, but I'll talk to them." She puts her lips tight together and nods her head twice, letting me know she's going to give them heck.

"If you want to," I say. "But I don't want any trouble."

Chapter 4

The following week, I look for Jimmy at the lunch court as I walk toward our favorite spot, the short brick wall, away from the Senior Court where all the footballers hang out. But I don't see him anywhere.

As I sit and wait, I begin to think about when me and Jimmy met in middle school. One day after school, he asked me over to his house. Jimmy lived with his divorced mother, Ms. Diaz, in a two-bedroom apartment near our house. She was nice to me, always offering me something to eat.

Once she offered me a piece of pie, but I said, "No, thanks."

"Are you sure? When you get home, you're going to wish you said 'yes.'" She was right. Boy, I bet the pie was tasty.

She gave Jimmy extra homework to do because she said, "Mijo, you're going to college."

So, he read a lot of books that he would give to me when he was finished: fun books like Tom Sawyer and some others about nature and science. After I read them all, I gave them back to him. Then we sat around and talked about what we read. Jimmy was really smart. I would help him study SAT vocabulary words with flash cards.

"Your turn," he'd say to me. "You've got to learn these words, too."

Jimmy is like that. He is always pushing me to do my best. I like that about him. He is a good friend. He is in the tenth grade accelerated classes. Students, like Jimmy, who score high on their IQ tests, are placed in the "Gifted Program."

Jimmy is late. I can't figure out why. He is usually here before me. I wait and I wait. He doesn't show up. It's weird.

Me and Jimmy have first lunch. My brothers have second lunch, so Jimmy is the only friend I have to talk to besides Sandra, but she always sits in Senior Court with her friends.

****

When I see Jimmy at practice I ask him why he wasn't at lunch.

"I got busy," Jimmy says. "I had something to do."

"Like what?" I ask. "Aren't you going to have lunch with me anymore?"

"Yeah, yeah, but sometimes," Jimmy says. "Sometimes I'm going to eat lunch with my girlfriend, Maria."

"Maria is your girlfriend?" I ask.

"Yeah, we're going steady," Jimmy says. "She wants to have lunch together, so you'll be on your own."

I can't believe it. I guess that's the way it is when a guy meets a girl, but I am really mad at him.

****

I'm bored eating lunch by myself for the last couple of weeks with no one to talk to. I pull a book out of my backpack and begin to read, but the noise and laughing makes it hard, especially today, Friday.

Fridays are school spirit days. Students get to do funny, weird things. Today the student body council declared it

"Pajama Day." All students can wear pajamas to school to show their school spirit and pride. But not everyone does. I wear my usual T-shirt and sweatpants.

I see Jimmy and Maria walk by a couple of times. He's in a pajama top and jeans. She has on zip up pajamas. They wave at me. But I don't wave back.

Then, Sandra, in pink pajamas, sees me and calls me. When she motions for me to come over, I walk towards her. She points up. One of the varsity guys had thrown her cheerleading pompoms into a small tree that grew in a planter near the bench where she sat with her girlfriends.

"Eddie, can you reach up there and get them for me?" she asks.

I don't say anything. I look up into the tree, climb on a bench, and stretch as high as I can to get Sandra's pompoms.

Then, as I reach up, someone pulls down my pants, showing my running shorts underneath. Everyone around begins to laugh really loud, except Sandra who covers her mouth with both hands.

I pull up my sweatpants with my weak hand and jump down from the bench with the pompoms in the other. I give the pompoms to Sandra.

"Thank you, Eddie," she says. "That's very nice of you."

I only nod. Then Sandra kicks high in the air, and with a rustling of pompoms above her head yells, "Go team!"

Then, I reach over and pull her pajama bottoms down below her knees. But nobody laughs. Sandra stands there in her pink underwear. Then she quickly drops her pompoms, pulls up her pajamas, and runs off, cinching the waist string as tight as she can. I bend over to pick up the pompoms, but before I could reach for them, one of Sandra's football friends grabs them away.

"Stay away from her you freak, you pervert," he says, pointing his finger in my face.

I walk away. I thought it was a game. I didn't think . . . . That's what Jesse says. I just don't think before I act. But I really thought it was a game. I feel so stupid. I didn't mean anything by it. I hope Sandra knows that. Damn, I get so angry at myself when I do stupid things like that.

****

After lunch, my fourth period teacher hands me a hall pass.

"Mr. Gonzales, the principal, wants to see you," he says. "Take your stuff. I don't know if you'll be back."

I pick up my backpack and head toward the office, wondering what to expect. When I walk inside, I stand at the long walnut counter until the secretary looks up from her desk and sees me. She has short brown hair and a pencil behind her ear.

"You must be Eddie," she says as she gets up from her desk and opens the swinging door. "Come around here, Mr. Gonzales is waiting for you."

When I go into the paneled room, I see several sports team trophies on the shelves, mostly football and basketball, but I do see a large cross-country trophy, too.

"Sit down Eddie," Mr. Gonzales says, pointing to the chair in front of his desk. "Do you know why I called you in?"

"No, not really."

"It's about the incident that happened at lunch today," Mr. Gonzales says as he rests his elbows on his desk and his chin in his clasped hands. He had short black hair and a dimpled chin. "It was reported that you pulled down Sandra's pajama bottoms. Is that true?"

"Well, yeah, but I didn't mean anything. I was just playing around."

"What do you mean playing around?"

"Yeah, you know it's Friday. Everybody was goofing around."

"Eddie, there is a difference between just having fun and exposing a girls underwear."

"I just thought . . . ."

"You just thought what?"

"I thought it was all part of a game. Someone pulled my pants down and everybody laughed. So I thought maybe Sandra did it. So I pulled her pajamas down as part of the game. Anyway that's what I thought."

"Eddie, you know I was in favor of giving you a chance here instead of sending you to Marshall High. But now, it's going to be difficult to explain to Sandra's parents what happened."

"Sandra's parents?"

"Yes, apparently one of Sandra's friends called home about the incident. Her mom called Sandra's mom. Sandra's parents are meeting with me on Monday."

"I really didn't mean anything."

"I know, but there will be consequences. Do you understand?"

"Yeah, I understand."

****

At home after school, I don't want to think about all the trouble I'm in. So, I think about when we were young, my brothers and me, all we did was read comic books. I mean we really read a lot of comic books. We had stacks of them over two feet high along the walls of our bedroom. We never threw any of them away. You name it, we had it. Superman, Batman, the Green Hornet, I'm telling you I could go on forever. But that's how I learned to read.

When I first started school, my teacher told my parents that I would never learn to read.

"He just seems not able to say the correct word," the teacher said.

But I was able to read. I just couldn't speak well. At home, I opened the comic books and read, but for a long time no one really thought I could read. They thought it was just me copying my brothers as they read, imitating sitting around, reading, and being part of them. It wasn't until they heard me giggle or laugh out loud that they began to think maybe I could read. I guess the turning point came when they heard me say in a loud clear voice, "kapow, zap, splat, kaboom." They all looked at me. Then they looked at the comic book that I was reading. There on the page they saw Superman socking Bizarro on the jaw and the words, "kapow, zap, splat, kaboom."

"Look mama," Jesse said. "Eddie is reading. He's really reading."

"Mijo, mijo," she said "You can read!" She gave me a big hug.

From then on, my brothers knew that there was something more to me than what I looked like and talked like. They really knew.

After a while, I read all the comic books faster than they did. I remember one day, when Jesse came home with three new comic books. Everybody jumped up and grabbed one and there wasn't one left for me.

"It's okay," I said. "I've got my own." I began to read an invisible book that I held in my hands. They all looked at me. I wet my fingertips and turned the pages like I was reading a real comic. They just laughed, a big laugh, and that made me feel good.

As I got older, I began to think about making my own comic book, my own comic book superhero. I imagined he would look like me, one strong side one weak side. One good hand, one bad hand. My superhero was known as Manny Vela when he was doing his regular job as an ambulance driver, but when asked, he became the "Fist of Fury." He is a righter of wrongs and fights against his arch enemy, Don Diablo. Fist of Fury is admired by all for his bravery and willingness to help those in need.

Then I think about Sandra and how I tried to help her, but everything went wrong. Now, because of her, I'll probably get kicked out of school. I wish I had never met her.

****

On Saturday, as usual we wake up early and head to the Sunny View car wash. Today we are very busy and short-handed. Me and my brothers try to pick up the slack, but it isn't easy. I'm working at the entrance of the car wash tunnel, sorting rags.

It's just before lunch when I see Jorge get into a brand new Cadillac and begin to wipe windows with clean rags. Jorge knows his job well. He has to move fast to keep up with the cars as they roll along the conveyor. But I see that he is sweating like mad, water dripping from his face like a leaky fire hydrant. I remember the time he got locked in a large trunk we found at the junkyard. We had to get him out with a crowbar. He was really scared and sweaty then, too.

Then, watching Jorge in the Caddy disappear down the end of the line, I see a big commotion. A lot of men stop working and surround a vehicle that had just come off the conveyor belt. I run over to see what's wrong. Inside the car, the Caddy, Jorge is frantically trying to open the door, but he can't get out. Everybody is shouting, trying to tell him how to unlock the newer automatic windows and doors. But when I look at Jorge's face, I see that he is near his breaking point. So I grab a towel, wrap it around my fist and start punching at the side window until it breaks into a hundred pieces. I pull Jorge out. Everyone gathers around as I sit on the ground holding his head in my arms.

"Are you okay? Are you all right?" I say.

"Yeah, yeah, I think so," he says. "I . . . I panicked. I thought I'd never get out of there."

When my brothers get to us, they are relieved to see that Jorge is all right. But when they look at the broken car window, they turn to me with a hard look and shake their heads. I know I'm in trouble.

After a while Jorge recovers, feels better, and keeps working until the end of the shift.

But when we get home, my brothers let me know that Mr. Ames, the owner of the car wash, is angry at all of us because he must pay the car owner for the broken window. Mr. Ames says that the cost of the broken window was coming out of our paychecks.

"Eddie, because you didn't wait for someone to open the door with the keys," Jesse says. "We won't be getting our paychecks for the next two months. If you had just waited instead of acting crazy, we wouldn't be in this mess. Thanks a lot!"

"Jorge was in trouble. I wanted to help him, to get him out. I didn't think. . . ."

"That's the problem. You never think before you act. You just . . . oh, forget it."

I don't say anything. I know Jesse and Jaime are really mad at me. I think they'll get over it, but I am wrong. They stopped talking to me from then on.

****

Asleep in my room, I hear "whir, whir, whir" in a dream. The sound sings to me in spinning circles around a void, an abyss, a spiral that draws me in like a hard-shelled nut falling into itself until it explodes in ribbons of color, violet, indigo, blue. Like a fever dream I had when I was a kid and father got mad because mother put me in bed with them and sang to me. I remember that far away melody like a whir.

I get out of bed, dress for church. All of us usually walk to church because it's close by. But today my brothers drive. My brothers leave without me. So, I walk with my mother. She likes to feel the sun on her face. When we get there, we sit in a pew next to my brothers.

I sit quietly thinking about the big mess that I'm in. At one point, I slide off my seat and kneel with my clasp hands on the back of the seat in front of me. I want to pray, but I can't think of the words to say. I need help. I need to find a way out of all this trouble I'm in. I bow my head into my clinched hands and begin, "Dear father in heaven . . . ."

After church I go to see El Indio. I tell him how everything seems to be messed up in my life right now. My brothers are mad at me, my friend Jimmy doesn't have time for me anymore, and Sandra and her parents are trying to get me kicked out of school.

"That doesn't sound good," El Indio says. "Sandra? I thought she was your friend. What happened?"

"Oh, I did something stupid. I can't talk about it," I say. "What should I do now?"

"Well, for one thing your brothers," he says. "Your brothers are your family. You are part of them. They are part of you. You must find a way."

"Oh, I don't know," I say. "Really, I don't need them. Sometimes I think I'm better off without them."

"Don't talk like that," he says. "I lost my brother. I know what it's like."

"What? Your brother Chaparro?" I ask.

"You asked me once what happened to him," he says. "I couldn't tell you then, but I can tell you now."

We sit on the wooden steps of his camper shell.

"What happened?"

El Indio stares out into the distance as if he were straining to see a bird in flight before it disappears into the horizon.

"Chaparro was proud to be a Raramuri," El Indio began. "And all of our family was proud of him because he brought honor and pride to our village whenever he entered the tribal running games with other Raramuri."

"Did you run with him?" I say. "Did you run together?"

"Yes, always," El Indio says. "We were only a year apart. When we ran, lots of people could not tell us apart. When Mr. Peterson came to our village looking for runners, everyone in the village pointed to us. At first, he was only interested in me. But I told him that I would go with him only if my brother came too. He agreed.

"After the Leadville marathon in Colorado, we were treated very well by Mr. Peterson. He was very proud of the first and second place medals that we had won.

"By then we were ready to go home, but Mr. Peterson had other ideas.

'I'd like to enter both of you in the Angeles Crest 100 Mile Marathon in California.' Mr. Peterson said. 'What do you think? '

"Chaparro looked at me. I was very willing, but I could feel that Chaparro was home sick and wanted to return to our family.

"I told Mr. Peterson that we thanked him for the offer, but we really must get home to our family, our village. Mr. Peterson said that he understood, but hoped we'd think about it because our running was drawing a lot of attention that was not only good for us, but for our village too. He explained that a lot of charity organizations got a lot more contributions when we ran. Those gifts of money were sent to help our people during the drought in Copper Canyon.

"I talked to Chaparro about it and realized that we would be helping our people back home if we stayed in the U.S. and ran more races.

"So, we agreed to go to California with Mr Peterson and enter the Angeles Crest 100 Mile Marathon. When we arrived in Wrightwood, California, where the race began, we were happy to see that the running course was high in the mountains, just like the trails we ran in Copper Canyon.

"At the beginning of the race, we were told that we didn't have to worry about wild animals and that the chaparral and manzanita were easy to avoid if you stayed on the path. Plus, one important thing, parts of the course must be run on the paved highway, so watch for cars and motorcycles, but most of all, watch out for falling rocks on the roadway because rockslides happen a lot.

"We were more than halfway through the Angeles Crest course ahead of all the runners when markers directed us onto the paved highway. Chaparro was setting the pace about ten yards in front of me. When we came to the roadway Chaparro looked back at me. I knew it was my turn to set the pace, so he dropped back, and I took the lead. We ran together beside the high granite cliffs to the right instead of the steep drop off to the left on the other side of the road. As I ran, I checked to see Chaparro running behind me about fifteen or twenty yards. There was a cool breeze that felt fresh and clean. Mr. Petersen said it came from the Pacific Ocean. An ocean we'd never seen.

About the end of the first half of the race, I realized I hadn't seen my brother for a while. At first, I thought for sure he would be catching up, taking his turn leading the pace. But as we reached the nine-hour mark, I became very worried about him. Something told me that something was wrong. I knew I had to run back up the roadway to find him. After running for a half hour, I saw his legs and arms sprawled on the side of the road below a steep rock face. I began calling his name 'Chaparro, Chaparro' but there was no answer. When I reached him, I saw his bleeding head. I looked around. I saw several large rocks and boulders scattered on the roadway. I knelt next to Chaparro. I held his head in my hands and yelled, 'Chaparro, Chaparro, wake up Chaparro,' but it was no use. He was not breathing. There was no life in him. I could see his racing vest was wet with his blood that spread across the word, 'Angeles.' I cried. All I could do was hold him in my arms and call his name. I cried and sobbed until Mr. Peterson spotted us as he cruised along in the support car.

"It wasn't till weeks after that I could even talk to anyone. I didn't want to get out of bed. I didn't want to eat. But Mr. Peterson took care of me.

'Are you ready to go back home?' he said. 'Your family has been asking about you. Wondering when you're coming home.'

'I can't go home,' I said. 'I can't.'

'Of course you can,' Mr. Peterson said. 'I'll take care of everything. You don't have to worry about a thing. I'll get you home.'

'I can't go home,' I said. 'I just can't.'

'Why not? Your family wants you home.'

'That's why,' I said. 'I can't go home because of my family.'

'What do you mean?'

'My family,' I said. 'My family, I promised them I would take care of Chaparro. That I would keep him safe.'

'But it's not your fault,' he said. 'No one could have foreseen this. It was a freak accident.'

'No, no it's my fault,' I said. 'Chaparro didn't really want to run here. He wanted to go home after the Leadville marathon. But I talked him into this.'

'Look, get a hold of yourself,' Mr. Peterson said. 'I understand you're in a dark place right now, but you do have to go home sometime.'

'I know,' I said. ' But I can't go right now. I need some time.'

'I understand,' Mr. Peterson said. 'Let me help you. You'll need a place to stay until you're feeling better. And I think I have an idea how I can help you.'

"That's when he brought me here to Las Lomas."

I don't know what to say. I feel sad. I put my arm around El Indio's shoulder.

"I'm sorry. I understand. I'll try harder to settle things with my brothers. I promise."

Then, out of nowhere, I remember the time I went with Jimmy and his mother to visit his dad in prison. That's what it feels like. Like El Indio is in prison. A prison of sadness and grief. He isn't free to go home, just like Jimmy's dad.

****

It was after practice one day about a month ago, Jimmy asked me if I'd go with him to visit his dad in prison.

"Look I haven't told anybody else about my dad," he said. "But I know I can trust you. He's in prison. He's been there for a while. And, well, my dad wants to meet you because I talk about you all the time when I visit him."

"What do you mean?"

"My mom takes me to visit him twice a month. Do you think you can go with me in two weeks? My mom must get permission for us to go."

"Geez, I don't know," I said. "Sure, Jimmy, I'll go with you. I'll ask my mom, but I'm sure it'll be okay."

"Great, thanks."

When we arrived at the prison the next Saturday, we waited in line to get checked in. The officers checked our ID's and gave Ms. Diaz a pass and pointed to the door to the visiting room. It was a large open room with tables and chairs set out with four chairs on each side of the table. Several uniformed guards stood along the blank white wall that enclosed the room. At one end of the room there was a podium where another officer stood, watching. As we entered the room, an officer directed us to a table at the far right and told us to wait for Jimmy's dad to arrive.

Then a side door opened, and Jimmy's father walked toward us. He wore a short grey-sleeved shirt. I could see tattoos all over his arms. He was muscular and had black hair like Jimmy's. Ms. Diaz and Jimmy stood up and waited for him. When he was close enough Ms. Diaz reached out her two hands and held his for a moment. Jimmy was able to lean across the table and give his dad a quick hug.

"Hey, Jimmy, so good to see you," his dad said. Then he looked at me and said, "You must be Eddie."

"Yeah, Eddie, that's me," I said as I stood up, reached out, and shook his hand. Then we all sat down together.

"I remember Jimmy telling me about you in the seventh grade," he said. "Jimmy told me that some guys were hassling him at school, but he wasn't worried because you were looking out for him."

"Yeah, I guess that's right. In the seventh grade I was, you know, bigger, taller than the other guys. So, they were kind of afraid of me."

"And you've been friends ever since, right?"

"That's right. But you know Jimmy has helped me out of a lot of messes too."

"What do you mean?"

"Well, I guess, some people think I'm weird. You know with my twisted leg and and arm."

"They make fun of you?"

"Sometimes, but if Jimmy hears about it, he gives them hell, I mean, heck. He's always been a good friend to me."

"And you've been a good friend to him," he said. "I wanna thank you for that." He looked with a smile in Jimmy's direction. " Hey, it looks like we'll have enough time for a quick game of chess. Jimmy, get the chess set from the bin. Eddie get us some sodas from the machine over there."

Jimmy and I got up and walked away, leaving Ms. Diaz and Jimmy's dad alone to talk for a while. I could tell that even though they were divorced, they were still friends.

Chapter 5

The following week at school, I wait every day for the summons to the principal's office. I know it's gonna be bad news.

Finally, on Thursday in second period, I hear coach Led call my name. I walk to his desk in the front of the class. I had asked coach Led to let me change my seat to the back of the room away from Sandra. Maybe that's why he calls me? Whenever I see her on campus, I turn and walk away. But sometimes from a distance, I catch a glimpse of her. It seemed like she was smiling and waving at me. I look away. I probably am just imagining it. Coach Led hands me a hall pass.

"Eddie, the principal wants to see you," he says. "But before you go, lets step out into the hallway so I can talk to you."

In the hallway coach Led puts his hand on my shoulder and says, "I know what this is all about, moving to the back of the room. Sandra has talked to me about it. She's very upset because you don't talk to her anymore. She wants you to know that she tried to talk her parents out of it. She told them that it wasn't your fault, but they didn't listen to her."

"She did?" I ask.

"Yes, she did. She values your friendship."

"I didn't know . . . ."

"Good luck, Eddie," coach Led says as he walks back into the classroom.

****

Mr. Gonzales' secretary lets me into his office, but he is not there. I sit in the chair in front of his desk and look around the room. He has a framed copy of his diploma from USC on the wall. Besides team trophies he also has lots of books on the oak shelves. The large window to the right has blinds that are closed. On his desk I see his name plate and the title underneath, "Principal." I don't like being in his office for a second time.

"Hello, Eddie," Mr. Gonzales' voice comes from behind me. "Sorry, I'm running late," he says as he sits at his desk across from me. "How are you Eddie?"

"Okay, I guess."

"As you know I had a meeting with Sandra's parents on Monday." Mr. Gonzales clasps his hands behind his head and leans back in his chair. Then he exhales a big breath and leans forward, grasping his arm rests.

Then I watch him slowly open a manila folder on his desk.

"I have reviewed progress reports from all of your teachers," he says. "You've been doing well in all of your classes since the start of school. Coach Ledesma says that you are an important part of his team."

I wait for the bad news.

"It's a shame. A real shame, Eddie," he says. "But I have no choice. You remember the last time we met I said that there will be consequences for your actions. Eddie, I'm recommending transfer for you to Marshall High. Of course. I will meet with your parents and inform them about this."

"Transfer?" I say. "I'm being kicked out?"

"Eddie, you're not being expelled," Mr. Gonzales says. "This will go on your record as a transfer. Marshall High has more resources to fit your needs."

"How long do I have?" I ask. "When will I be transferred?"

"It'll take a few weeks," Mr. Gonzales says. "As I said, I need to talk to your parents, file the paperwork, and wait for a vacancy at Marshall High."

****

On Sunday I go to see El Indio because I have nobody else to talk to. My brothers are still giving me the cold shoulder. They're still mad about losing their paychecks. I meet El Indio at the gate.

"I'm getting kicked out of school," I say as I hand him an old paint can someone left for him at the gate.

"What happened?" El Indio says. "Dimé. Tell me every-thing."

"Sandra's parents made the principal transfer me to Mar-shall High. They're kicking me out of school."

"I'm sorry to hear that, Eddie," he says. "When? When is this going to happen."

"I don't know, in a few weeks I guess."

"That's too bad."

"Yeah, everything is all messed up." I sit with El Indio on his camper's wooden steps. We sit there in silence for a long time. It is like that with El Indio. He is able to just sit quietly with me until I find the words to let him know how I feel. "I don't know if I wanna go to school anymore at all. I don't have any friends. Nobody talks to me. It's like they don't see me. They walk by me, but really don't see who I am."

"Eddie, don't think like that," he says. "You've got to go to school. What about cross-country? You're part of a team."

" They don't need me." I say. "What's the point? I'm being kicked out. I don't want to go to practice anymore. I'll be leaving the school soon."

"Eddie, you know you love to run," he says. "You can't quit just like that."

"But you don't get it," I say. "What's the point of practice, of running at all, when I'm being kicked out of school."

"I'm sorry to hear that," he says. "I hope you'll change your mind."

I have nothing else to say and I'm about to leave when El Indio stands up and asks me to go to the warehouse with him.

"I need some help," he says. When he opens the warehouse door, I see the far wall where someone had begun to paint over the mural with white paint, El Indio's mural of Copper Canyon.

"What's going on? Who did that?"

"I did," El Indio says. "I need your help to finish. I need to cover the wall with white paint."

"What? But why, why?"

"Mr. Peterson has sold the warehouse."

"Really?"

"Sí, and I will be going home to my family."

"What? You're going home to Copper Canyon?"

"Sí, I need to go home. My family has been waiting for me."

"No, no," I say. "El Indio, you're the only friend I have left. The only one I can talk to. You can't go."

"Eddie, you knew I had to go home sometime," he says as he looks into my eyes. " You knew I couldn't stay here forever. I'm sorry, but I must go home to my family."

I feel my cheeks getting hot and my eyes begin to water. I suck in a deep breath full of pain. I turn away from El Indio and run as fast as I can through the gate onto the trails of Las Lomas.

After running in the hills for hours, I go home as the sky gets dark. Usually, I feel much better after running, but not today. I feel worse. I feel sad and lost. I go into the house and head for my bedroom.

"Where have you been, mijo?" mother says. "Your supper is getting cold."

"Yeah, where were you?" Jesse asks. "You're always sneaking off, going somewhere."

"None of your business," I say. "I like it better when you don't talk to me."

"Sure you do," Jaime says. "So you can keep all your little secrets to yourself."

"I wasn't talking to you," I say, giving him an angry look.

"Boys, boys, stop," mother says. "Eat, eat."

****

At school I sit in the lunch court by myself away from everyone. I watch the seagulls fly in the air and land on the roof of the auditorium like a line of robbers ready to attack, snatching fries, cheese cubes and apples slices that students leave behind when the bell rings at the end of lunch period.

"Hey, Eddie," Jimmy calls to me as he comes close to where I sit. "Hey, man, how you've been?"

"What's it to you?" What do you want? Your girlfriend not here today?"

"Eddie, come on man, I'm still your friend," Jimmy says. "I heard about you being transferred. I thought maybe you'd want to talk about it."

"Yeah, but not to you."

"Come on, Eddie,"

"Jimmy, just leave me alone."

"Okay, okay, I'm going," he says. "I'll see you later at practice."

"Don't count on it."

"What do you mean?"

"I won't be at practice. I quit the team."

"What? Quit the team?"

"You want to do something for me, then tell coach Led I won't be coming to practice anymore."

"But Eddie . . . ." Jimmy reaches out his hand toward my shoulder.

I brush it away, walk off, and leave him standing there by himself.

****

The next day in second period as I enter the room and start to walk to my desk down the rows, I feel a tug on my shirt sleeve.

"Hi, Eddie," Sandra says. "Eddie, can we talk later?"

I look down as she sits at her desk waiting for an answer. I can't think of anything to say. And when I look at her, it brings back the memory of what happened, of what I did, about the stupid thing I did. I feel embarrassed and can't talk. I turn away from her and walk to my desk at the back of the room.

At the end of the day I skip practice and take the bus home. In my bedroom I put on my running shoes. Then I hurry out the front door to Las Lomas, thinking that maybe running would help me out of this sadness. I run along the high ridge above El Indio's camper shell. I stop at the guard rail for a few minutes and watch him at his cutting board, fixing something to eat with his machete. I sit there for a long time without him knowing. After a while I see him go into the warehouse with paint brushes and paint cans. It hurts to think about the work he is doing inside.

When the warehouse door shuts, I know this is the last time I will ever see him. I stand up, my eyes watering, and run as fast as I can uphill, trying my hardest to outrun the hurt and loneliness I feel creeping over me.

****

Over a week passes without a word from the principal about my transfer. My father tried his best to change the principal's mind, but when he heard what I did, he couldn't argue anymore. So my transfer to Marshall High is a sure thing. I just don't know when it's going to happen. I begin to think that maybe it's for the best. I don't belong here. Nobody wants me here.

During lunch I find a new place to sit by myself away from everyone. Sandra and Jimmy get the message that I just want to be left alone. I stop going to practice. I stop visiting El Indio. At work, I do my job and stay out of trouble.

At home, my brothers talk about practice that day and how they are getting ready for the league championship meet in a couple of weeks. They laugh together when they remember the funny stories coach Led told that day. I feel left out, but I know it's my choice.

****

The next day in class, coach Led passes the test out. We all groan.

"Tell us about your running at USC," Sandra says. "I heard you had the record time for running the two-mile."

"Nice try. Wait. That's an idea," coach Led says. "I'll make you a deal, if everyone in the class finishes this test early, I'll tell you about my running days at USC."

Sandra is good at getting people to talk. I'm not surprised that coach Led goes along with it. He likes to tell stories. And all of us like to hear his stories.

"Okay, then, everyone is done!" Coach Led says after about forty minutes. "So, I have about ten minutes to tell you the story of my running days.

"As you can see, I wasn't one of those real muscular sprinters. I was a long-distance runner. I was skinny. All the newspaper coverage always described me as the lean-built runner. Anyway, at six-foot one inch, I had a long stride and plenty of lung power. I think it was from my boyhood in Northern California, running between the rows of grapes vines growing on the hillsides.

"It's only been about a year and a half since I competed at the collegiate level. I made a name for myself by breaking the school record for the two-mile. I was lucky enough to run it under nine minutes.

"But it didn't take long before another runner came along and beat my record time.

"I guess the sad part of the story is that I had a chance to be on the U.S. Olympic team, but it didn't work out that way.

"First you must understand that a runner must wear the best shoes possible. Shoes must fit the runner's feet perfectly. And shoes must be replaced every three hundred miles or so. But I made the mistake of running with borrowed shoes. My teammate, Tom, loaned me his shoes at the last minute before a race because my laces on both shoes broke.

"As a result, I ruptured my Achilles heel and aggravated my runner's knee. You see, Achilles heel is an injury that happens when you wear shoes that don't fit properly.

"Does anyone know where the name Achilles heel comes from?"

"I think it's a Greek myth," Sandra says. "Achilles, as a baby, was dipped in a sacred river to make him strong. His mother held him by one heel, and sure enough his body was protected, except where she held him by his heel."

"That's right Sandra," coach Led says. "So, my Achilles heel injury prevented me from practicing or competing in a race for several weeks, that, along with my runners' knee, made it impossible for me to be on the U.S. Olympic team."

"What did you do?" Sandra asks.

"I had to accept it and move on. After I graduated, I entered a teaching program. I became a teacher instead of a runner. It all worked out for the best. I love my job!"

Rinnnng! At the bell, everyone gets up to leave.

"I need to talk to you," coach Led says when he sees me heading out of the classroom. "Meet me after school at the track. You don't have to run if you don't want to. But let's talk."

****

At the end of the school day I walk toward coach Led as he watches the team warming up before their practice runs.

"Thanks for meeting with me, Eddie," coach Led says. "I've heard a lot of things, but I really would like to hear from you what's going on. Why aren't you coming to practice anymore?"

"What's the use of being on the team, of practicing when they're going to kick me out any day now."

"I understand how you feel," he says. "But for weeks now I've noticed in class that you've been down, actually looking pretty sad about something. What else is going on?"

"I don't know, coach." I try to hide my feelings from him, but I can't. "I don't have any friends, and my brothers are mad at me. What am I gonna do? I don't belong here anyway."

"Things will get better. You have to believe that. You know I want you on the team. I want you to come to practice. I need you. The team needs you."

"I don't know. It's like I've hit a wall, you know how you talk about running really hard and things are going great, then you hit a wall. What can I do about it?"

"You stop, rest, gather yourself, and keep running."

When I hear my coach's voice, it's like I've heard his words before. In my mind, I see my Uncle Edmundo and I hear him say to me, "The stuff that's in the way is the way."

"Coach can I ask you something?" I say.

"Sure, you can."

"What does it mean when people say, 'stuff that's in the way is the way?'"

"I've heard that before," coach Led says. "I can only tell you what it means to me. For me, sometimes the obstacle becomes an advantage and offers an opportunity.

"An opportunity?"

"Yes, a chance to do greater things."

"Oh."

"What that opportunity is for each person, no one knows, but if a person can accept what stands in his or her way, then that person has found the way," he says.

I stood quietly for a long while.

"So, what do you think? Are you running with us today?" he says.

"Yeah, I'd like to."

"Then what are you waiting for? Your team is about to start the course. Go!"

I put my toe on the line with the other team members. Jimmy smiles at me. Coach Led blows the whistle and we take off to the path leading into the bramble.

Pretty soon I'm on my own at the rear, but it feels good to be back. As I run, I think about how my teammates made me feel welcomed, like I never left. Jimmy is a good friend to me. To have friends, I think, you must be a good friend. As I run, I feel lighter and lighter. My stride quickens. I'm not sticking to the ground anymore. I feel like I'm flying.

When I come out of the bramble, I see all my teammates waiting for me. Jimmy hands me a bottle of water and pats me on the shoulder.

"Good to see you back, Eddie."

Chapter 6

The next day in second period, I walk up to coach Led's desk. He sits hunched over his roll book as the students walk in.

"Coach, can I move my seat back up to the front like before?" I ask.

"Sure, go ahead," he says, partially covering a grin with his hand.

"Thanks."

I sit in the empty desk next to Sandra. I smile at her.

"Hi, Eddie," she says with a small wave of her hand.

"Hi, Sandra," I say as I look at her across the narrow aisle.

"Eddie, I've got something important to tell you," Sandra says. She scoots her desk closer to mine. "Maybe we can talk later at lunch? Okay?"

"Sure, yeah, let's talk at lunch."

****

"Eddie, Eddie," Sandra shouts it at me from across the lunch court and waves at me to come over. I walk over to where she is sitting with her girlfriends. They are all dressed up in their cheerleading uniforms and pompoms. As I get near, she stands up and walks toward me.

"Eddie, let's sit over here," she says. "I want to talk to you in private."

We sit down on a bench by ourselves.

"I know you didn't mean anything by it," she says. "It just took me by surprise. I guess I was embarrassed. I guess I was kind of mad, too. All my friends said that I should dump you. You know, not talk to you anymore. But after a while I thought about it, and I knew that you wouldn't do anything to hurt me on purpose. I tried to explain it to my parents, but they wouldn't listen. I'm sorry. It's just a big mess."

"I'm sorry, too. It's all my fault." I can hardly look her in the eye.

"It's okay, but I want you to know that the football guys have started a petition."

"A petition? For what?

"Eddie, they want people to sign the petition to get you transferred to Marshall High," she says. "But don't worry, nobody will sign it. I don't think."

"You don't think? Maybe . . . ."

"Let's forget it," she says. "I have some good news!"

"What is it?"

"All of us, all the cheerleading squad is going to be at your cross-country league final next Friday," Sandra says. "We'll be there to cheer you on."

"Really?" I say. "I'll let coach Led and the team know you'll be there for them."

"We're going over to the gym to work on our routines right now. See you later," she says as she starts to leave.

"Before you go," I say. "I need to know you forgive me."

"Sure, of course."

"I just want to say that I'm sorry, again," I say.

"It's okay. Forget about it."

"Really? Thanks a lot," I say. "Maybe you can help me with something? You know Jimmy, my best friend, Jimmy. I need to say 'sorry' to him too, but I don't know how. What should I do?"

"He's your best friend, so maybe you could do something nice for him and I'm sure he'll understand," Sandra says. "Gotta go. Good luck."

****

On Friday when the lunch bell rings, I run with my paper lunch bag to the table in the lunch court where they're selling balloons for spirit day. I buy a red balloon and sit at my favorite spot on the low brick wall. Pretty soon everybody comes pouring out of their classrooms heading for the lunch court or the cafeteria. I keep an eye out for Jimmy and his girlfriend Maria. When I see them coming out of the cafeteria, I yell at them to come over. They both look at me with big smiles and head my way, holding hands.

" Hey, Jimmy. Hey, Maria," I say as I reach out to Maria and give her the red balloon tied to a string. "Maria, Jimmy wanted me to get this for you. So here."

"Thanks, Eddie," she says.

"Don't thank me. It was Jimmy's idea," I say, winking at Jimmy. "You guys wanna sit with me while I eat my lunch?"

"Maybe," Jimmy says. "But only if you're going to share some of those homemade burritos your mother makes for you."

We laugh together as the balloon floats above our heads. Maria's brown eyes are focused on Jimmy. She holds on to Jimmy with her hand on his arm. She's a thin girl who always wears wide belts around her slim waist.

"How's Sandra?" Maria smiles and gives Jimmy a slight elbow bump.

"Sandra? Okay, I guess. Do you know something I don't?"

"You know she's on my cheerleading squad and I know she looks out for you."

"Yeah, I know."

"It hasn't always been easy for her."

"What do you mean?"

"We've been friends since middle school. She was in foster care until she was adopted when she was ten years old. She had a tough time fitting in."

"I didn't know."

"Anyway, she really likes you."

"I like her too. She's a good friend to me."

After a while Jimmy and Maria leave to buy more balloons.

****

I was up all last night trying to think of something I could do for my brothers to make up for the mess I made at work. But I couldn't see what I could give them to make up for loosing their paychecks. I want them to know that I am sorry. I want to give them something of mine to make up for it. But all I could think of is the secret I have that they don't know about. Then it hit me. That's it. That could be my gift to them.

"Hey guys," I say as I sit with my brothers in Jessie's car waiting for the car wash gate to open. "I've got something to tell you. You know how I kind of disappear sometimes on Sunday after church? You're always asking me where I go, but I've never really told you the truth. But I want you to know now because you're my brothers."

"What?" Jesse says, turning his head and sitting upright. They are all listening now.

"I go visit El Indio. We spend time together, just talking."

"No way! Are you crazy?" Jesse looks at me to see if I am lying. "He'll chop you up into little pieces with that machete of his."

"No, he's a nice guy and he's a runner too, just like us. He's a long-distance runner."

"Are you for real?" My brothers can't believe what they're hearing.

"I think you'd like him. Do you wanna meet him, talk to him?"

"Are you kidding? Sure, count us in." Jesse and my brothers smile at me and pat me on the back.

"But here's the thing," I say. "He needs some help painting the warehouse. His boss, Mr. Peterson, sold it. El Indio will be leaving soon. I'll be going over there on Sunday to help him out. Do you want to come with me?"

"Yeah, sure, we can help," Jesse says as the others nod in agreement.

****

On Sunday, me and my brothers head up the road to the gate where El Indio lives. At first, looking through the gate, we don't see El Indio anywhere.

"Where is he?" Jesse asks.

"He's gotta be here somewhere," I say. "I don't think he's left for home yet."

Then we see the door to the warehouse open. El Indio steps out with a paintbrush in his hand. He looks in our direction, but doesn't say anything.

"El Indio , these are my brothers," I call to him. "Will you let us in?"

El Indio walks slowly toward the gate, unsure what to do.

"We came to help you," I say. "We came to help you paint."

El Indio grins , opens the gate, and lets all of us in.

"Hi, Eddie," he says, "Your brothers?"

"Yeah, Jesse, Jaime and Jorge," I say. They shake El Indio's hand. He smiles at them.

"Okay, sí, if you really want to help me," he says, putting his arm around my shoulder. "Follow me. I'll show you what needs to be done."

After he opens the door to the warehouse, he leads my brothers and me to the back wall where we see the mural scene.

My brothers don't say a thing, but their jaws fall open and their eyes become wide as they look up at the peaked mountains, forests, and rivers that are half covered by wide brush strokes of white paint.

"That's Copper Mountain," I say. "That's where El Indio lives."

"Wow!" Jesse says.

"El Indio painted it to remind him of home," I say. "But now it has to be painted over. El Indio is going home."

After El Indio hands us paint cans and brushes, he leads us to the tall ladders that lean against the wall. We work together in pairs. One of us climbs up the ladder as the other one holds it steady. We paint for the next four hours until the entire wall is like a white sheet of paper and Copper Canyon is no longer visible.

When we are finished, El Indio leads us out of the warehouse into the afternoon sunlight.

"Can you stay a little longer?" he says. "I want to give you something to eat before you go."

"Sure, we can," I say. "That sounds good."

We sit on wooden boxes around the makeshift plywood table. We watch as El Indio brings out small crates of fruit and vegetables from the camper. He sets them on the table. Then he brings out his machete from a black leather sheath at his side. When little Jorge sees it, he falls off his box backwards. We all laugh.

"I'm not gonna hurt you," El Indio says. "I'm going to cut up some watermelon and cantaloupes for you guys."

We sit and eat the ripe fruit with El Indio, feeling tired, but satisfied.

"Eddie says you are a long distance runner," Jesse says when we are finished eating.

"Sí, that's true," El Indio says. "I ran the Colorado Leadville 100 Mile Marathon not too long ago."

"One hundred miles," Jesse says. "And we complain about our cross-country course of two to three miles long."

"What did you place?" Jesse asks.

"I came in first place."

"Wow, that's something."

"Would you like to see my medal?"

"Yeah, we would all like to see that," I say, seeing the eager looks on my brothers' faces.

El Indio gets up from the table, walks to his camper, and returns with a small box in his hand. He sits at the table and puts the box down. Then he slowly opens it. Inside we see a large round gold medal tied to a red white and blue ribbon. The gold is inscribed with "Leadville 100 Marathon — First Place."

"That's really something," Jesse says. "I've won some cross-country medals before, but nothing like that. Do you wear special running shoes for a marathon like that?

"No, only what I always wear," El Indio says. "I wore the same shoes that I run with at home, huaraches. Here, take a look. I'm wearing them now." El Indio stretches his legs from beneath the table.

Jesse looks down at El Indio's feet that are tied with leather straps attached to old rubber tire soles.

"You ran a hundred miles in those?" Jesse shook his head. "Do they grow wings and let you fly?" All of us laugh and point to El Indio's huaraches.

"Algunas veces, only sometimes." El Indio grins.

El Indio passes the medal around to each of us to get a better look. Then he gets up from the table and walks back to his camper with his medal.

"Well, I think we better go," I say. "Are you ready?" I look at my brothers.

When El Indio returns, we thank him for the food as we walk toward the gate.

As we get near the gate, El Indio puts his arm around my shoulder and says, "It's good to see you with your brothers. I'm glad you found a way."

Once outside the gate, we wave goodbye to El Indio. Then we walk home in silence.

****

At home we sit at the dinner table. When my father is home for dinner it's his custom to have each of us report what's going on in our lives. It's part of his training he says. Father was in the Marines, and it shows. He makes sure our mother covers the dinner table with a red and white checkered tablecloth. In the middle of the table sits a mustard bottle, a ketchup bottle, and napkins.

Father asks Jorge to report first.

"This older woman, like a grandmother," he says. "I helped her out of her car and when her car was ready, I helped her get in. I didn't think much of it, but then she lowers the window and gives me a five-dollar bill."

"That's nice Jorge, keep up the good work," father says. "Are you saving your money?"

Jorge nods yes.

"I've got a big test tomorrow in geometry," Jaime says. "I really gotta study hard tonight."

"Good, do that," father says. "And you'll do fine."

"I don't have anything to report," Jesse says. "Everything is just rolling along, things are fine."

"De veras," father says. "You're a lucky man, but remember hard work beats good luck every time." Then father looks at me.

"Well, I'm kind of . . . ," I say. "I'm worried, really worried."

"You haven't heard from the principal?" father asks. "It's been a couple of weeks now."

"No, I haven't heard a word about my transfer," I say. "I hope that I can run at the meet finals next Friday."

"Only time will tell," father says. "Don't worry about it. It is what it is."

****

"Can I borrow your hat, Eddie?" Jorge says as he walks into the bedroom before bedtime.

"My hat, sure," I say. "Where are you going?"

"Nowhere." Jorge looks away.

"Then why do you need my hat?"

"For school, when I go to school tomorrow."

"What? You don't need a hat for school," I say. "What's wrong? What's going on?"

"I need the hat when I go to school so nobody will see my lousy haircut."

"Dad's marine crew cut. Kids making fun of you?"

"Yeah."

"So what. Don't let it bother you."

"I can't help it. They all point at me and make fun of me."

"They aren't your friends if they do that."

"Yeah, Oscar, he's my good friend. He backs me up."

"That's it. That's all you need is one good friend to stick up for you."

"Yeah, but it bothers me what they say."

"What do they say?"

"They call me melon head."

"What?"

"You know, 'Pelón, pelón, cabeza de melón.'"

"Don't worry about that. You look them in the eye and say, 'You know what. I'm proud of my haircut. I've got a great haircut. You're just jealous.'"

"Really?"

"Yeah, really. When I was younger, your age, I used to walk around with my hand in my pocket so nobody would see how it looked. And my foot, I used to cross my legs every time I sat down in a chair so nobody would see how crooked it was. But do you know what, after awhile I thought, 'It's my hand and it's my foot. It's part of me. This is who I am.' Now I don't walk around like that anymore. I don't sit like that anymore. I am me, so that's the way it is."

"Really?"

"Yeah, really. And Jimmy is my best friend. He sticks up for me, too."

"Like my best friend, Oscar."

"Yeah, so, do you want my hat?"

"No, I don't think so, Eddie."

"Don't worry. Your hair will grow back," I say. "Anyway, when you get to high school, Dad will let you cut your hair anyway you want."

Chapter 7

"Are you excited about Friday?" Sandra says as she leans toward my desk in second period class. "We've been working on our routines. We're ready to go."

"Well, that's great," I say. "But I'm really worried about Friday."

"Worried?"

"Yeah, I don't know if I'll be here on Friday," I say. "I might be transferred out before then."

"Oh, don't worry," Sandra says. "Things will work out. I'm sure of it."

"How can you be sure?"

"I don't know," she says, lowering her eyes. "You're right. I really don't know."

Just then coach Led calls me to the front of the room. He hands me a slip of paper, a summons to the principal's office.

When I enter Mr. Gonzales' office, I see him standing at the window looking out into the lunch court area in front of the auditorium.

"Eddie, have a seat," Mr. Gonzales says as he turns around.

I sit in the chair and kind of brace myself for the bad news by holding onto the arms of the chair as tightly as I can.

"Your transfer date is firm," he says. "You'll be going to Marshall High a week from today, Monday."

"Does that mean I can run at the league finals this Friday?" I ask.

"Yes, you can run."

"Really? Thank you so much Mr. Gonzales. I really appreciate it."

"Coach Ledesma said it's important that you are there. Thank him. He really wants you to be part of it. He said that your Frosh/Soph team has a good chance of winning the league title. Good luck to you and your team."

****

On Thursday before the meet, coach Led calls the team together in the locker room at practice after school.

"Listen, you guys," he says. "You've worked really hard this week preparing for the meet and now tomorrow will be the payoff."

All of us are silent, some sitting on the narrow benches and others leaning against the lockers. We can all feel the importance of this moment. We are a team. Coach Led is our leader. We know that what he has to say will make a difference tomorrow.

I especially feel grateful to him for speaking up for me and letting the principal know how much he wanted me to run in the league finals meet. I'm not one of his gifted runners who have some of the best times in the league. I'm not even a finisher, coming in as one of the five places in a race. But I believe him when he says that I am an inspiration for the whole team. I run the course with my hobbled leg because he says it is important. And I want to be part of something, something bigger than me, part of a team. A team that wants me there just because, because I am important to them. And by running, doing my best at every meet, on every course, I am giving back, letting them know that they are important to me, too.

"This is how I see it," coach Led says. "Varsity has a great chance of coming in first and winning the league championship. JV has five strong runners whose times are among the best in the league. Frosh/Soph for sure has a shot at the league title. Jimmy has the best time in the league and his teammates are close behind."

Smiles spread across the locker room like wildfire. My teammates feel confident and proud.

"Now let's not get ahead of ourselves," coach Led says. "You know our strategy. We run from behind. We let them set the pace, but we push them, keeping close. We stay behind until we're ready to make our move and take the lead. The other schools like to run from the front, but that's not us. We save the best for the last and we will do it again tomorrow."

Everyone is on their feet.

"Let's have a great practice today," coach Led says. "And I'll see you at the team dinner tonight at my house at 6:30. Okay, let's hear it."

Coach Led stretches his hand in front of him and all of us join in, setting hand upon hand and shouting, "Go Eagles!"

****

Coach Led lives with his wife in a small three-bedroom house near the school. We all get to his house at the same time. It is a team tradition to load up on carbs before a big meet. So, coach Led hosts a spaghetti dinner for the team.

We all enjoy the camaraderie and the last-minute pep talk from the coach. After dinner outside, we sit around in the patio as the coach stands in front of us and begins his talk.

"Remember the basics," he says. "Pace yourself! Not too fast at the start when your adrenaline is kicking in. Don't sprint uphill but move fast downhill under control and keep your momentum for as long as you can."

Everyone gives an understanding nod.

"And tomorrow, three hours before the race, only carbs — bananas and peanut butter sandwiches. No meat or dairy. Got it?" he says.

"Got it!" The whole team answers.

"And, since we're the home team, we're expected to help with setting up the course for tomorrow's meet. I want to see everyone there right after their last class. There will be plenty to do."

****

On Friday the team meets with coach Led on the track next to the course. He is sitting on the chair next to a six foot table with several clipboards in front of him. Each of the clipboards has a work assignment — pop-ups, cones, golf carts, chalker.

"Listen up, you guys," coach Led calls out. "Each of you sign up on one of these clipboards to get your assignment. Then when you hear your name called out, follow the groundsman who will show you what you need to do."

There is a big commotion at the table as everyone tries to figure out what clipboard assignment to take. Of course, everybody wants to ride in the golf carts to deliver equipment, but placing the pop-ups to shade the officials, setting out the cones to mark the course, and chalking a white line to indicate the correct course path are important tasks, too.

I let everyone get to the clipboards and sign in before me. It didn't make a difference to me what I did as long as I could help. Finally when the dust settled, I reach for a clipboard, but coach Led's hand gets to it before me.

"Eddie, I want you to help me," he says. "The officials will be arriving soon and I need help checking them in. Here, sit in the chair next to me. Here's a list of their names. When they arrive, I'll call out their names and you check them off the list."

I sit in the chair next to the coach as he hands me the list of names of the officials. I can't believe how many officials are needed to run this meet, but I guess, a meet of this size, with four different schools represented and over one hundred runners, needs a lot of manpower. The list includes judges, a time keeper, a starter, umpires, funnel judges, results recorders, and paramedics in case of a medical emergency. Eventually all the officials are accounted for and checked off the list.

"Good job, Eddie," coach Led says. "That's it. When your teammates are done with their chores, call them together on the track. I need to talk to the team about today's race."

"Yes sir."

Soon busloads of runners begin to arrive from the different league schools: Wilson, Century, Bassett. Each team finds a spot to gather together on the field. We huddle around our coach on a grassy stretch near the starting line.

"Okay, harriers, this is it," coach Led says. "Before you warm up, I want you to remember a couple of things. You know as well as I do that our course is a tough one, but we're used to it. Even still, it's going to test your physical and mental stamina. Your lungs are going to burn and your legs are going to hurt. Just keep going. Remember, run inside on a turn, run in a pack, if possible, make a move on turns and on downhills to pass." He looks into our faces. "Oh, one more thing, the Frosh/Soph team will be running short with only six runners because Bobby has the flu and won't be with us today. But that shouldn't be a problem. We only need five of you to cross the finish line. Any questions? Then, let's do it."

Coach Led extends his hand. We make a tight circle around him, and our hands meet his, "Go Eagles!"

After warmups, I hear the field announcer call out the start of the Frosh/Soph race. The first race of the meet. My team gathers around the coach for last minute instructions.

"Okay, boys," coach Led says. "You've worked hard for this. Now is the time to give it all you've got. It doesn't matter that we're shorthanded today. You've got some of the best times in the league. I know you can do it. Fly Eagles!" He claps his hands and points to the starting line.

We head toward the officials who are standing in place. Then, the six of us walk to the starting line. The white line is not long enough for each runner from the three schools to put his toe on the line. So, each team is assigned a "box," a small section of the chalked starting line where each team member lines up one behind the other. I take the last spot on our team. My best time for the two-mile course is twenty-one minutes and fifty-one seconds. All my teammates run it in under sixteen minutes. Jimmy has the the best time of ten minutes and twelve seconds.

"Get ready!" The starter's bright orange sleeve goes up and he points the gun straight up into the sky. Then, for about thirty seconds, an eerie silence freezes all movement and deadens all sound, not even lungs are breathing.

"Bang!"

A wave of runners rolls out in front of me, heads bobbing and elbows moving like pistons, down the cinder track for about twenty yards. Then, the tide turns toward the dirt path leading to the opening in the bramble where runners thin to four alongside each other. I follow with my giddy-up gait, good leg forward, twisted leg coming from behind. The dust from the sprinters' feet rises like steam before me, but I know what I must do. What I've always done, head for home, the finish line, as fast as I can.

As I come up on the milkweed to my right, I can still see some stragglers making their way. But as soon as I approach the palo verde tree, I don't see anyone. At this point, the path curves to the left as I get near the start of a long hill. When I reach the top, I let the downward momentum carry me until I can spot the castor bean leaves in the distance.

That's when I see Jimmy, down on one knee, looking white as a sheet and holding one hand to his chest.

"Jimmy, Jimmy," I call out as I come near. "Are you okay? What's wrong?"

Jimmy doesn't speak as he falls to the ground on his back. I kneel down beside him and call his name "Jimmy, Jimmy," but he doesn't answer. His eyes are closed. He isn't moving. I bend down close to him, but I can't hear or feel his breathing. I stretch out his legs and put his arms to his side. "Jimmy, Jimmy," I call again, but no answer. I know what I must do. I thump the middle of his chest hard with the soft heel of my palm. Then I begin to press down on his chest five times. Next, I breathe air into his mouth and watch for his chest to rise. Then I begin pumping his chest again. I repeat my routine many times until finally, when I go to give him air, his eyelids flip open, his eyes roll up, and he makes a sound like rushing wind.

"Jimmy, Jimmy, can you hear me? "

"Eddie," he whispers.

I put my arm around his shoulders and set him up right.

"Jimmy, we've got to get some help. Can you stand? Can you walk?" I say as Jimmy looks up in silence.

"Jimmy, I'm going to help you stand up and carry you out of here." When I get Jimmy to his feet, facing me, I wrap my arms around his waist, lock my good hand onto my weak one and lift him as high as I can on my strong-side shoulder, like a sack of potatoes, and begin to run like I've never run before. My feet are flying as I head out of the bramble toward the finish chute where I know there will be help.

Waiting at the finish, groups of cheerleaders, parents, and students, are all watching in silence, not believing what they are seeing — me running with Jimmy on my shoulder. Coach Led runs toward us as I kick up chalk dust at the finish line.

"I've got him," coach Led says. "Give him to me, Eddie. I've got him." Coach Led takes Jimmy from my shoulder and carries him like a baby to the the nearest table where he sets him down. "Jimmy, Jimmy, can you hear me?"

"Yeah, coach."

"Somebody get a blanket and call the paramedics over here, now!"

"What happened to Jimmy?" Sandra says as she takes my hand, leads me to a bench and sits me down.

"I don't know," I say. "I found him on the ground, not breathing, so, so . . . . Is he all right?"

"Yeah, coach Led has him," she says. "The coach is taking care of him."

When the ambulance comes, the paramedics check Jimmy over, put him on a gurney, roll him into the back of the ambulance, and speed off.

"Eddie are you all right?" coach Led says as he walks toward me. "Eddie, tell me what happened to Jimmy."

"I found him, on the ground near the stand of castor beans. He wasn't breathing so I thumped his chest and gave him CPR like I learned in health class."

"Eddie, you may have saved his life," coach Led says, patting me on the shoulder. "Quick thinking. Good job!"

"Is Jimmy going to be okay?" I ask.

"Yes, he's on his way to the hospital for a full check-up. Eddie, wait here while I go call Jimmy's mom and Mr. Gonzales and let them know what happened."

Just then three judges and the results recorder come rushing up to coach Led. I can't hear everything they're saying, but it sounds like there are a lot of questions about the results of the Frosh/Soph race. Finally, coach Led shakes hands with the four men and hurries away to make the phone calls.

Sandra stays with me until coach Led returns. My teammates come by, shake my hand, and say "We did it! Thanks, Eddie!"

When coach Led returns he has a big smile on his face.

"Jimmy's mom is headed to the hospital. I told her what happened. She said to tell you thank you. Mr. Gonzales said that he wants to see you first thing Monday morning in his office before you report to Marshall High."

"Okay, coach," I say. "The team, the guys came by . . . how'd we do in the race?"

"You haven't heard?" coach Led says. "You and your teammates are the league cross-country champions! They owe it all to you. You see, your teammates placed one, two, three and four, but without a fifth finisher, we would have to forfeit. You crossed the finish line under your own power and saved us. Not only that, our team's combined scores were the lowest, giving us the win!"

"What?" I cover my eyes so no one will see me cry. Then, after taking a deep breath, I look up. Sandra smiles at me and puts her arms around me, hugging me tight.

"Go, Eddie," shout the cheerleaders as they gather around me and kick high into the air, holding their pompoms above their heads.

Chapter 8

On Sunday I run up to Las Lomas to say goodbye to El Indio who is leaving for home today. And I really need to let him know what happened on Friday.

"El Indio, it's me. Let me in," I shout.

"Hola, Eddie," he says, stepping out of his camper with a big smile on his face.

After he opens the gate for me, I can't help myself and I give him a big hug with both arms wrapped around him so that he couldn't move.

"Hey, what's going on?" he says.

"I've got so much to tell you. I don't know where to begin," I say.

"Dime, tell me everything," he says. "From the beginning. Here let's go sit down on the steps."

As we walk over to the wooden stoop, he puts his arm around my shoulders.

"Well, you know we had a big league meet on Friday." I say as we sit down.

"Yes, the final meet of the season."

"Yeah, that's right. Well, something terrible happened during the race."

"Tell me."

"My best friend, Jimmy, fell down on the course because he had chest pains. But nobody knew. Nobody could see what was happening to him. The arroyo bushes hide everything. But when I came up the path, I saw him. He was on one knee, white as a ghost and hurting. At first, I couldn't believe what I was seeing. Then Jimmy fell over, passed out cold, and didn't move. I ran up next to him and knelt. I called his name, but he didn't say anything. So, I gave him CPR the way I learned in class. Then he came to and I carried him to the end of the course. They took him to the hospital and said that I saved his life."

"Eddie, Eddie!" El Indio throws his arms around me and begins to cry.

"What's wrong, El Indio?" I can't move in his tight hug. "He made it. The doctors said that he's gonna be all right."

"You did a good thing, a great thing." El Indio lets go of me and brushes the tears from his eyes. "I'm proud of you. Wait here. Don't move." El Indio stands up and goes into his camper. "Here, I want you to have this. You deserve it," he says when he comes back.

He opens the small box in his hand and takes out the Leadville gold medal. He puts the red, white, and blue ribbon around my neck. "Stand up. There, it fits you just right!"

At that moment I begin to cry. I don't know why. And El Indio begins to cry, too. I stand there and I feel like a winner, a real winner, for the first time in my life.

Then from behind us we hear voices and laughing. When we turn around to look, we see my three brothers sliding down the slope from the road above.

"Hey, you guys," I say. "What are you guys doing here?"

"We wanted to say goodbye to El Indio," Jesse says as all three of them dust off their clothes and walk toward us. "Wow, Eddie, did El Indio let you wear his medal?"

"Yeah, he gave it to me!" I hold it up so my brothers can see as they gather around. "He said that I deserved it for helping Jimmy."

"That's so cool!" Jesse looks at El Indio. "We have something for you. A going-away present." Jesse hands El Indio a shoebox tied with a blue ribbon. "Open it."

El Indio slowly unties the ribbon, opens the box, and begins to smile. He reaches in and brings out a pair of new huaraches. "Gracias."

"They're just like ours," Jesse says as he points down where El Indio sees that all my brothers are wearing huaraches, too. "Now we can fly when we run, just like you."

We all laugh. Then El Indio sits on the step and puts on his new shoes.

"Guys, I'll wear them always," El Indio says. "Until they wear out and I can't fly no more." He gets up, walks over to my brothers, and puts his arms around their shoulders. "Look," he says as he casts his eyes downward. "We can all fly together. Com'on Eddie, you can show us how."

Just then we hear a blue Ford honking at the gate.

"It's Mr Peterson. He's come to pick me up, to take me home," El Indio says as we follow him to the gate.

After Mr Peterson drives in, we all help El Indio pack his few boxes into the car.

El Indio shakes our hands all around, says goodbye, gets into the car and drives off with Mr Peterson.

I watch El Indio wave from his window, slowly disappearing down the road.

Chapter 9

On Monday, I walk into the principal's office. Mr. Gonzales meets me at the door and holds out his hand for me to shake. I look around the office and see Jimmy's mother sitting next to the principal's desk on the right and sitting next to her is another couple. I see coach Led standing with a broad smile on his face.

Mr. Gonzales leads me to a chair and asks me to sit down as he walks to the other side of his desk.

"Eddie, let me introduce you to Mr. and Mrs. Willis, Sandra's parents," Mr. Gonzales says. "This is Mike Willis and his wife, Cheryl Willis. You already know Ms. Diaz, Jimmy's mom, and, of course, you know coach Ledesma. Eddie, I called you in today to let you know that I have rescinded your transfer to Marshall High. You'll be attending this school, your school, for as long as you want.

"I can still come here, to Arroyo High?" I can't believe it.

"That's right, and that student petition about you has been withdrawn by the students," Mr. Gonzales says. "And these good people here wanted to talk to you themselves, personally, about how they feel. Ms. Diaz, would you like to start?"

"Hi, Eddie," Ms. Diaz began. "I know you've heard this from me before, but I'm so thankful that you were able to help Jimmy. I can't thank you enough. You saved his life. I'm sure of it. He had a heart defect that no one knew about. If it wasn't for you and your quick thinking, well I don't know . . . ."

Ms. Diaz gets up from her chair with tears in her eyes and walks toward me. I stand. She hugs me. I hug her. After a minute or two she smiles at me and sits down again.

"I think the Willises have something they would like to say to you, too," Mr. Gonzales says.

"Our daughter Sandra has always spoken very highly of you," Mr. Willis says. "We, my wife, and I, weren't so sure. We were pretty upset about the incident at lunch. But I want you to know, now that we have all the information, that my daughter was right, you are a very outstanding young man. You deserve to be at this school. And this school deserves to have you. So, we both wish you the best of luck in all that you do." Mr. and Mrs. Willis stand up and walk toward me. I walk toward them. Mr. Willis shakes my hand very firmly. Mrs. Willis gives me a hug.

"Thank you, thank you," I say.

"Now, coach Ledesma please let us all know the big plans we have for spirit day and the Pep Assembly this Friday." Mr. Gonzales says.

"Eddie, we're going to celebrate a lot of things on Friday. The Varsity team won the cross-country league championship and your team, the Frosh/Soph team, won the league championship in their division, but most importantly we're going to celebrate you."

I notice that coach Led's words get stuck in his throat a bit and his eyes become watery.

"You're a genuine hero, not only to us, but to the whole school and we want you to know it." Coach Led moves toward me. I stand up as he put his arms around me. I put my arms around him.

"Thank you," I say, not sure if all that's happening is real.

****

On Thursday, the day before the assembly, I wake up in the morning remembering the dream I had last night. In my dream I was flying, flying out from the car wash tunnel into the sky, flying without effort. Wherever I pointed, I flew in that direction. I felt so happy. I told myself in the dream to remember how it feels so that I can teach my brothers. When I looked down to the earth, with the eye of an eagle, I could see my father, my Uncle Edmundo, and El Indio standing on the ground below, looking up and waving at me.

That evening, I sit in my room a bit worried about what it's going to be like, you know, the assembly. Will I have to say something? What exactly is going to happen? I'm excited, but worried, too.

"Mijo, I've ironed your white shirt," mother says as she comes into my room. "You have to wear your suit tomorrow. You must look your best. I'm so proud of you."

"Thanks, mom." I hug her and hang the shirt in the closet next to my suit coat and pants.

Then my brothers come rushing into the room, pulling, and tugging at one another, trying to get to the shoe rack before the other one.

"Hey, you guys," Jesse says. "There're two shoes. Each one of you can take one. You don't have to fight about it."

Then Jaime and Jorge look at each other and pick up one of my shoes. They begin to spit shine them with a cotton rag twisted around their index finger dipped in a tin of black Kiwi Wax.

"What are you guys doing?" I say. "Those are my shoes."

"We know," Jorge says. "We're going to shine them for you. The best shine you've ever seen."

"You're going to look your best tomorrow," Jesse says, "For sure."

"Yeah, you're right," I say.

"How's Jimmy doing?" Jesse asks.

"He's good. I talked to his mom," I say. "His heart operation went well. He's recovering in the hospital. She knew about the assembly Friday and says Jimmy wishes me good luck."

"Good to hear."

"You know, Jesse, I've been thinking."

"Thinking about what? "

"About El Indio, I wish he were here. That he could be at the assembly tomorrow."

"Yeah, he'd like that."

"So, I was thinking," I say. "Maybe I could wear his medal tomorrow at the assembly."

"That's a great idea," Jesse says. "You should do it."

****

On Friday, as I sit on stage with coach Led waiting for the assembly to begin, the other coaches and my team members arrive. Looking out into the empty auditorium, I notice six double-door entrances. I see the perforated white acoustic panels on the walls and the big overhead lighting that show the old sixty's decor. The tiered fabric seats are in alternating school colors, gold and blue, marking the seating sections.

Then the doors open, and hundreds of students jostle down the carpeted aisles to their assigned seats, filling the auditorium like a helium balloon ready to burst. I watch the excited students sit at the edge of their seats, waiting. Suddenly, down the aisles come cartwheeling, short-skirted cheerleaders led by Sandra and the marching band with sparkling brass horns ripping the air and booming big bass drums everywhere. On the stage more cheerleaders wave dozens of yellow and blue pompoms, invisible twirling batons, and too many, large, table-cloth-size flags on tall sticks, whipping through the air. I listen to the clamor and roar of fight songs and shrill-voiced cheers that climax with a clash of brass cymbals as large as manhole covers. The thundering, exaggerated beating of kettledrums on stage makes my heart pound and my spirit soar. I sit nervously rubbing El Indio's medal that hangs around my neck.

After the pledge of allegiance, Mr. Gonzales walks to the podium. He taps the mic once, twice to make sure that it's working. Then the auditorium is silent.

"First of all, I'd like you all to welcome a very special guest today who would like to say a few words, Ms. Diaz."

Jimmy's mom walks to the mic, turns, and smiles at me.

"I'm here today to thank all of you from me and Jimmy for all your good wishes, flowers, cards, stuffed animals, and balloons. It really helped make Jimmy feel better and he can hardly wait to get back to school with all of you. Thank you, all!"

Applause fills the auditorium as Ms. Diaz returns to her seat.

"Today is a very special day," Mr. Gonzales says. "We're proud of all our athletes and their achievements." A cheer goes up with some whistles and some hoots.

"Also, it's a special day because we are here to honor one of our own, a cross-country runner whose quick thinking and action on the course saved the day. Eddie, come over here."

Clutching my medal with one hand, I walk to the podium as Mr. Gonzales presents me with an engraved plaque.

"Eddie Santos, I am honored to present you with Arroyo High School's Hero Award."

I take the plaque in my hands and look out into the auditorium where everyone is standing, clapping, and cheering. I raise the plaque above my head as the cheering grows louder. Then, the band plays our alma mater with trumpets, bass drums and cymbals in motion as the audience sings, filling the auditorium with heart-felt song and loud, goose-bump-making music.

Now, for the first time ever, music is in my life, played by people I know, and they know me, just like I thought it always would be.

"You're a winner! You're a hero!" says coach Led as he comes up behind me and puts his hands on my shoulders.

Suddenly, my teammates lift me on their shoulders and chant, "Eddie, Eddie, Eddie." Then, the crowd looks up and shouts, "Eddie, Eddie, Eddie."

I feel like I'm flying.

****

At dinner that night, my brothers, my father, my mother, and my abuelita sit around the table and I feel grateful for many things. As my father bows his head and blesses the food that we are about to eat, I think about El Indio and how proud he would be of me. I know at this moment that I succeeded in something that people who know me, and some that don't, would always remember me by. I have a family and friends who love me for who I am.

www.ingramcontent.com/pod-product-compliance
Lightning Source LLC
Chambersburg PA
CBHW050739150726
48196CB00003B/274